The Pig Did It

The Pig Did It

JOSEPH CALDWELL

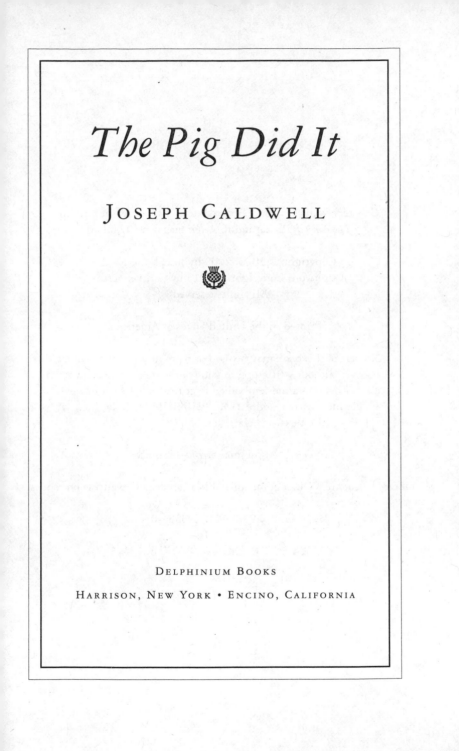

DELPHINIUM BOOKS

HARRISON, NEW YORK • ENCINO, CALIFORNIA

Chapters from this work appeared in slightly different form in
The Antioch Review and in *Ambit* magazine (London).

Printed in the United States of America

Designed by Jonathan D. Lippincott

Library of Congress Cataloguing-in-Publication Data is available on request.

ISBN 978-1-8832-8534-0

22 23 24 25 26 LSC 10 9 8 7 6 5 4 3 2

To
Robert Diffenderfer
. . . and about time, too!

Author's Note

The reader should assume that the characters in this tale, when speaking among themselves, are speaking Irish, the first language of those living in the western reaches of Ireland where the action takes place. What is offered here are American equivalents. When someone ignorant of the language is present, the characters resort to English.

The grave's a fine and private place,
But none I think do there embrace.

Andrew Marvell,
"To His Coy Mistress"

The Pig Did It

1

Aaron McCloud had come to Ireland, to County Kerry, to the shores of the Western Sea, so he could, in solitary majesty, feel sorry for himself. The domesticated hills would be his comfort, the implacable sea his witness. Soon he would arrive at the house of his aunt, high on a headland fronting the west, and his anguish could begin in earnest.

Through the bus window now, Aaron could see that the pasture land of Ireland had been long since parceled out, the stones put into service as defining walls, creating what looked like a three-dimensional map, each border drawn in heaviest black, each territory a rectangle or rhomboid with an occasional square or triangle thrown in to vary the cartography.

On the upper slope of an unshaded hill a flock of sheep was slowly nibbling its way to the west as if clearing a path to the sea. Bunched together, a cloud of their own making, they concentrated on their appointed task, uncaring for whom the path was meant as long as the job put food in their stomachs. Above the flock, about ten feet from the nearest sheep, there was a shepherd, a man—or maybe a boy—wearing a sweater of wide horizontal stripes: reds, green, blue, gold, and closest to the waist, black. He was holding a crook, a shepherd's crook. Antiquity lived. Customs survived. A whole history of the ancient land was being offered for his amazement. But Aaron was allowed no more than a few seconds to marvel at the gift he'd been given. It was not a shepherd's crook. It was a furled umbrella, which the man propped against a rock, pulling a camera from the pouch at his side to take a picture of a sheep. He was no more a shepherd than Aaron was. He was a tourist at best, a government bureaucrat at worst.

The bus, more comfortable and modern than the Greyhounds and Trailways at home, sped along at what Aaron judged to be about fifty miles an hour, down the narrow road that curved and wound its way through and around the Kerry countryside. It would bring him by late afternoon to the village—a cluster of a few houses and a pub, Dockery's—where his aunt Kitty would meet him and drive him the rest of the way to the old fieldstone house where he'd spent summers as a boy, equally unwanted by his newly divorced mother and father.

He loved the house, set as it was in a field not far from the edge of a cliff that dropped to the sea. Below was a beach that stretched along the ocean's shore before ending at a rock face that rose from the sea itself and walled off the cove that lay on the farther side. When he'd stayed with his aunt and her family, he'd resented the wall, a barrier between him and the sandy shoreline of the cove. It separated him from the other children who could come to swim and wade in the quieter waters, to bury one another in the sand, and to build forts and castles that, had they been real, would surely have saved the land from the plundering foe that had swept down from the north and driven his ancestors all but into the sea.

But now the memory of the wall pleased him. His stretch of beach would be deserted. His solitude would be inviolate, his loneliness unobserved and unremarked except by the sea itself. There would, of course, be gulls, there would be curlews. He would hear their shrieks and watch the curve of their spread wings riding a current of air so rarefied that only a feather could find it. Perhaps there would be cormorants and, if he was lucky, a lone ship set against the horizon. There would be squalls and storms, crashing water, and thundering clouds. Lightning would crack the sky. Winds would lash the cliffs and—again, if he was lucky— rocks would be riven and great stones thrown into the sea. Then he, Aaron McCloud, would walk the shore unperturbed, his solitude, his loneliness, a proud and grieving dismissal of all that might intrude on his newly won sorrows.

Aaron had been unlucky in love. And now his body and his soul, trapped in perpetual tantrum, had come to parade their grievances within sight of the sea. Surely the rising waves would rear back in astonishment at his plight, cresting, then falling, bowing down at the sight of such suffering. Solemn would be his step, stricken his gaze. Only the vast unfathomable sea could be a worthy spectator to his sorrows. The culminating act of Aaron McCloud's love for Phila Rambeaux would soon come to pass at this edge, this end of the ancient world.

At thirty-two Aaron had given himself permission to fall in love—or so he thought—with a woman inordinately plain, a student of his in a writing workshop at the New School in New York. She had undecided hair, mostly straight, but more frizzled than curled at the ends, halfway between brown and blond, the actual coloring left to whatever light might get caught in the unmanageable mass. Under the fluorescent glare of the classroom, she was blonde; in the muted light of the lobby, she was brunette. Her eyes were hazel, flecked with green, and for cheeks she had been given flat planes that slanted down from her eye sockets to her jaw. Her mouth consisted of a squat isosceles triangle, her nose a straight and common ridge, her chin uninflected, undimpled, a serviceable meeting place for the bony angles of her jaw.

But she had notable, beautiful hands, the hands of a harpist. Aaron had the feeling that if he were to press one of those hands to his face, the scent would be not of soap or expensive lotions but of some subtle balm secreted from within the hand itself, enthralling and mysterious. Yet for reasons unknown Aaron was inflamed not by the hands but by the face, the flat cheeks, the flecked eyes, the serviceable chin. His amorous urges were sustained as well by her habit of playing with her right ear whenever she was talking.

Her writing was wispy. She had an inborn antipathy for the specific, mistaking the obscure for the ambiguous. She lacked vulgarity, that gift most needed to transform intelligence into art. She'd been given no artistic equivalent to her notable hands.

And so, two years after his wife's elopement to Akron, Ohio, with a baritone from the choir of Saint Joseph's Church, Aaron decided to let his favor fall on Phila Rambeaux. How grateful the woman would be. She would be given the attentions of a man not without assets, a man noted for his easy charm, his easy wit, his easy allure. He was a published novelist and the recipient of several awards obscure enough to be considered prestigious. For his classes he had more applicants than he could accept. For his socializing he had more friends than he could accommodate. He owned a floor-through apartment in a brownstone on Perry Street in Greenwich Village. And, more important, he had a trim and taut physique, not the product of a grueling vanity that required a personal trainer, but maintained by a native restlessness—bordering, some said, on the manic. Also, he could cook.

Phila would be a pushover. Aaron's lovemaking would drive her to the edge of dementia, making rescue necessary, a rescue he would effect with reassuring kisses, a consoling embrace characterized by withheld strength, followed by the reviving ministrations of whispered invitations for yet another journey to the boundaries of madness. He would even, when the right moment came, confess that for her, and for her alone, he had decided to free his sexuality from the confines to which he'd committed it when the baritone had made off with Lucille, the soprano. For Phila, and for Phila alone, he had encouraged the resurgence of his heretofore disciplined carnality. Restored to the fullness of his manhood, ardent with awakened lust, aching with a resuscitated tenderness, he made his move.

But Phila Rambeaux was not about to be pushed over. When invited for coffee, then for a drink, then for dinner, she didn't so much refuse as convey her perplexity. She seemed not to have the least idea what he was talking about, as if he had introduced a subject so alien as to preclude intelligent comprehension. If he had asked her would she like to harvest cocoa beans in the Congo, she could not have given a more bewildered "No, thank you." The offer of a movie, then a play, then an opera, was met by the same confused response, neither annoyed by his persistence nor curious about his intent. The very idea of his existence outside the classroom was so far beyond her powers of perception that her incomprehension was absolute. He was not so much dismissed as dissolved.

Aaron did, however, get her to come to a reading of his new novel by making it a class assignment. She attended but was gone before he could wade through the crush and distinguish her by his attentions. As a last resort he gave a party in his apartment, inviting all the students. Phila came, wearing a dress of black silk with orange and blue geometrics that looked like intergalactic debris left behind by a failed space probe. When he asked if she'd stay to help clean up, Aaron was given a perplexed shake of the head as if cleaning up were an idea foreign to her understanding. It was, however, when Ms. Rambeaux left, laughing, in the company of the single student in Aaron's class who could claim any talent, one Igor something-or-other, that Aaron was seized by the Furies and taken into torments never before visited upon the human psyche. And so the party ended.

Then the semester was over, and Phila Rambeaux was accepted at a writers' conference in Utah. The recommendation he had written for her specified that she had no talent—whatsoever—obviously the conference's most compelling prerequisite. And so she was off—gone for good. Aaron would not wait for her return. He would pack up his anguish and haul it off to Ireland. He would carry as well his resurgent unappeased sexuality; he would gently lay, alongside his comb, his toothbrush, and his deodorant, a determination never to repeat this folly. Women had had their chance. There were limits to his munificence, and from now on those limits would be strictly observed. All this he brought to Ireland, to County Kerry, to the shores of the Western Sea.

"Pigs! Pigs!"

Aaron heard the taunt through the heavy glass windows of the bus. Two teenagers coming toward them on their bikes repeated the cry as they wheeled past the windows. "Pigs! Pigs!" Aaron didn't doubt that this was some social commentary aimed at those who sat passively and were carted comfortably from one place to another in adjustable, upholstered seats. "Pigs!" The shout faded in the distance. Aaron twisted in his seat to catch some final glimpse of the insolent bikers, but they were gone. The only other movement among the passengers was a general straining not in the direction of the hostile youths but toward the front of the bus. A man in a heavy tweed suit snorted, the sound not unlike that of the animal just mentioned. A young woman closed her book and studied her fingernails. Those in the aisle seats leaned sideways for a clearer view ahead. A tall skinny man got up and went to the front of the bus. His hair, whitened with what seemed to be zinc oxide, rose in stiff spikes from his scalp. He was wearing a leather vest over a red silk shirt, his pants a pair of baggy blue sweats, and his shoes the obligatory untied Reeboks. The youth peered through the windshield, blocking the view of anyone else who might want to take a look up ahead.

The driver had slowed the bus and by the time they had rounded a curve, Aaron understood the bikers' cry. There, crowding the road, were the pigs, a mob more than a herd, each squealing and screaming as if the destined slaughter were already under way.

A few pigs were now clambering up the rock walls that lined the roadway, others trotting up the hills, with about four of them sniffing the wheel of a truck stuck in a ditch. One of the front wheels was still spinning, as if the truck's fortune, for better or worse, would be made manifest at any moment.

The bus stopped; the door opened. The spike-haired man was the first off, then the driver. With some pushing and shoving of their own—as if taking their example from the pigs—the passengers, Aaron included, emptied the bus. A frail elderly woman elbowed her way to the front with all the courtesy and consideration of a fullback.

The round-up of an escaped pig is not a spectator sport. Almost without exception the passengers were wading in among the pigs or running along the road, clapping their hands, calling out, *"Suuee! Suuee! Suuee!"* A young woman with a switch pulled from the nearby thicket was trying to herd the pigs together in the road and move them in the direction the bus and the truck had been going. She was, Aaron noted, a bit too self-consciously costumed as a swineherd in her baggy black woolen pants and thick woolen sweater, dark gray, spattered with the rust colors of earth, the green stains of crushed grass, and a few purple streaks of unknown origin.

And yet, to Aaron, she seemed more a dancer than a keeper of pigs. Her sneakered feet managed to escape being dainty, but only just. And their quick pivots and graceful turns allowed him to guess with fair accuracy the easy movements of a most feminine form that not even the outsize clothing could begin to conceal. Then, too, her auburn hair would be flung across her face, first one side, then the other, suggesting a happy abandon hardly consistent with her present predicament, revealing in intermittent flashes the eyes, nose, mouth, cheeks, chin, and neck of a woman of vital beauty and immediate allure.

She was laughing, clearly enjoying herself to the full, as if a ditched truck and a mob of confused pigs were one of life's more surprising delights. With each flick of the switch she would let out a small cry of triumph, a point scored in a game that provided unending amusement. The pigs, in return, raised their snouts and screamed their indignation.

One of the passengers, an elderly woman, had made her way into the middle of the clamoring beasts and was slapping their snouts and spanking their hams, more intent on punishing their behavior than restoring order. The man in the tweed suit ran along the side of the herd, yelling, clapping his hands over the pigs' heads, sending even more of the frightened animals off into the pastures that lined the road. The zinc-haired youth had placed himself a few yards down the slope of a hill and had made it his job to see that no pigs passed into the valley below. Stamping a foot, shouting, hunching forward in warning, he did his best to encourage a return to the road; but, to complicate his task, more than a few of the pigs seemed attracted to his performance, and the youth, to escape their charge, was forced to move farther and farther down the slope, the pigs in pursuit, eager for yet more sport.

The man in tweed was running alongside a pig as it raced up a hill, a contest to see who would make it first to the top. Two passengers—ample matrons of great dignity whom Aaron had heard conversing only in French—were standing to the side, nodding their disdain, speaking to each other like sportscasters commenting on the game in progress.

Some pigs stood next to the truck, content to wait for things to calm down. Others rooted in the grass with their snouts, searching out whatever tasty grubs might be found beneath the turf. One pig, pinker than the rest, began prodding its fellows with its snout, bumping, shoving, grunting, and snorting even louder than the piercing shrieks of those whose dignity was being offended. Only when, with a few discreet sideswipes, it tried to force the two Frenchwomen into the herd did the swineherd, the beauty with the switch, put an end to its presumptions by driving it deep into the middle of the pack.

Merrily she flicked her switch, claiming with a quick nip one pig, then another, reminding each in turn that it belonged to her and might as well accept the happy fact. The woman's eyes, like the switch, seemed to flick and dart, rejoicing in the calamity, more interested in the chaos than in the rescue of her stock.

To show he wasn't a tourist, Aaron snapped a reed-thin switch from the bramble. With brutish disregard he stripped it of its leaves, swished it twice in the air like a fencing master testing his rapier, and looked around for a task worthy of his style and dash. He would pick one of the more wayward pigs and bring it safely back into the fold. Two were sniffing their way along the rock wall, another was already halfway down the hill toward the valley, three were trotting back to the road, their playtime at an end. One, on the upward slope, had raised its snout and was squealing, begging for rescue, another coming down the hill slowly, almost daintily, as if it had relieved itself in the gorse and didn't want anyone to know what it had been up to.

Aaron saw his pig. Or, more accurately, his pig saw him.

There, about twenty feet up the hill, it stood, its front legs brazenly spread to declare its defiance. Its huge head was thrust forward on a neck and shoulders that a bull might envy, its snout twitching, daring Aaron to come closer. The eyes, pink-rimmed slits, blinked, peered, then blinked again. The ears stiffened, the tail lifted, and from out behind came a big arc of piss, a sturdy yellow stream that, for some reason, made him think of Coors beer. Aaron, aloud, counted to three. The arc collapsed and disappeared. Aaron started up the hill, stick in hand. He would go around the pig, approach it from above, apply the switch, and drive the animal down to the road. As he went up the hillside, the pig turned, keeping an eye on him. Aaron kept moving, higher. The pig itself turned some more, still watching. By the time Aaron had arrived at the place from which he'd expected to make his attack, the pig had turned around completely. The two of them faced each other once again.

Aaron would tolerate no more. He stomped down the slope toward the pig, uttering a high and fearful yell that could have been mistaken for the cry of someone who'd seen a mouse. The pig, unimpressed, stood its ground. Aaron stopped. With the switch he made two quick slashes in the air. The pig blinked but didn't move. Aaron went to his left. He would charge from the side. But just before he could complete the maneuver, the pig, with a gruff snort, turned and made a dash up the hill. Aaron hesitated only a moment, not for decision but for adjustment to the shock. The pig was not cooperating. Then he sped up the hill, the held switch bending again and again like a divining rod bewildered that its divinations were being repeatedly ignored.

The pig continued up the hill, gaining speed as it broke into a full gallop. Aaron followed, determined now that the pig would not escape. Just below the summit, the pig veered to the left and started toward the eastern slope that curved around to the other side of the hill. Aaron gained slightly, but he began to worry about how long his breath would hold out. He wasn't exactly panting, but he could tell that the breaths were becoming shorter and shallower and there was a slight stitch in his right side. Heart attack or appendicitis, either could fell him at any moment, but he no longer cared. He would get the pig.

For its part the pig was covering ground at a fair clip. To Aaron it seemed that it was deliberately leading him, luring him farther and farther away from the bus, from the road, from his fellow passengers, like Moby-Dick, tempting him into uncharted territory, to a hidden valley beyond the hill. If that were its aim, Aaron would become the pig's Ahab, his will more steeled than ever in spite of the panting breaths and the ache in his side.

The pig disappeared around the eastern slope, bounding over the heather, avoiding the rocks. Aaron followed, putting the switch into his left hand so he could hold his side with his right. He rounded the curve. There, higher up toward the summit, stood the pig. It was rooting up the turf with short grunts of repellent satisfaction. Aaron stopped. He stood there panting. The ache in his side had grown to an actual pain. He let the switch fall from his hand. He turned and headed back the way he'd come. He would have no more interest in the pig. He cared not at all that it was being abandoned on the hillside, that it must forage for itself as best it could, denied the amenities of a safe clean pen, the swill-filled trough, the privilege of being counted among the chattel of a woman with a surprised laugh and darting eyes.

Aaron completed the turn around the side of the hill and began the descent. From this height—he hadn't realized how high he'd climbed—he could see to the west the parceled pastures that sloped upward, unheeding of the edge of the cliff that dropped off to the sea. The town to the north was gray even in the slanting light of the lowering sun, the houses, stucco and stone, obviously on friendlier terms with the hills than with the cliffs and the sea. On the horizon, a single ship seemed about to drop sideways off the end of the earth. No fishing boats, no curraghs could be seen. The coastal waters had been fished out long before. The hulking rock of Great Blasket Island, more than a mile off-shore, rose into a cloud as if hoping to find in its mists the meaning of its hard existence.

Aaron picked up his pace but still had to brake each step so he wouldn't slip and slide down the steep incline of the hill. His aunt Kitty would be waiting, and she was not a woman famous for her patience. Fortunately she and Aaron were—through the generational peculiarities of the McClouds—near contemporaries, with Kitty, two years older. As children they had allied themselves to each other more as cousins than as aunt and nephew. Only in a clinch would Kitty bring into play the precedence decreed by her having been sired, in his old age, by Aaron's grandfather. She was the final fructification crowning more than thirty fertile years that had produced seven children, two clusters of three each, with nine years intervening, and then, at the last, this ultimate flowering who would, to the family's chagrin, inherit the house, chattel, and pasturage of a doting, dotaged father, a deliberate perversion of primogeniture leaving all not to his eldest son but to his youngest daughter. Encouraged by this perversity, Kitty soon fell into a habit of exasperation, an inability to understand or accept inconvenience. Spoiled, she considered herself to be without blemish and had no patience with anyone who took a different view, not because they were wrong but because they lacked discernment.

Aaron liked her and always had. It was she who had taught him to be, like herself, a little snot. She had schooled him in the ways of intractability; she had inspired in him a scorn of negotiation or compromise. They got along fine. Still, she would not want to be kept waiting—even for him. Aaron's apprehensions were not without cause.

He continued down the hill but stopped when the entire scene, himself included, was put into shadow, but gently, like a whisper. The town darkened, and the sea become still. Only the tops of the clouds, those out over the island, held the light, bright streaks of blazing silver. Eager for the day to end, a cloud had come up from the sea, from beyond the western horizon, claiming the sun for itself, leaving the land and even the sea to do as best they could under its shadow. The world seemed abandoned, forgotten, as if in the moment ages had passed and he was being given a glimpse of the future, the land drained and empty, the sea sullen and indifferent.

Aaron felt the stirrings of an ancient fear, but before it could take its unshakeable hold, there welled up in him not so much a memory as a repeated experience, a distant moment, alive again not in his mind but in his senses. He was with his great-aunt Molly, Kitty's mother, an ample and hearty woman with a harsh laugh and a tender touch. They were climbing, through the heather, through the gorse, to a hill high above the town when, without warning, a mist rose up, obliterating the whole earth, separating them from everything known and familiar. He must have whimpered because, after letting out a short quick laugh, the good woman took his face between her two rough hands and said, "Poor child, you're not Irish at all, are you, not anymore. What has happened is the everyday miracle from which comes all our wisdom. We've been taken into a mystery. See? It's all around us and we know nothing but itself. Everything is mystery—and we accept it to God's glory. So give up being afraid. And be Irish again, for the moment at least. And wise as well. Learn—and fast—to live with mystery. And to die with it, too. Now let me kiss your foolish forehead"—which she did—"and you'll be afraid no more. And let me take your hand in mine and we'll go up the hill, not even expecting to see our way. It is ever so. And then we'll eat a bit of cake I've tucked into my pocket."

Aaron felt the kiss again on his forehead. He drew his hand across the place where her lips had touched, then looked down at his feet. The stirring of the childhood fear faded to nothing. And, better still, the pain in his side had receded, his breathing had been restored, the heavings of his shoulders no longer needed to keep him going. The cloud, having had its way, resumed its advance to the east, hoping perhaps to frustrate the moon somewhere over northern France. Light once more shone, the world restored to its vital near-somnolent self. Aaron raised his head. The stones of the town sparked with the minerals and ores that were their secret element. Whitecaps roused the sea, and the grass was given again not only its multiple shades of green but the scents as well of heather, gorse and, if he was not mistaken, nicotine.

But before Aaron could revel completely in the world's restoration, he saw that he had come down the wrong side of the hill. There were no pigs, there was no bus, there were no ineffectual herders scampering in the road. The woman with the darting eyes and the surprised laugh was nowhere to be seen. He would have to reverse direction and make his way back to the opposite slope. Just as he was about to make the turn, he found himself staring more intently at the road below. True, he could see no pigs, no bus, no passengers, nor the swineherd with the switch. But the truck was there, still in the ditch, as if taking a snooze before continuing on its journey.

He looked to the north and saw only two cars and another

truck. He looked to the south and could see nothing beyond the bend in the road. He ran down the hill; he leaped the wall; he stood in the road. There were pig droppings squashed into the asphalt. An apple core and a banana peel lay on the white stripe that served as a median; there were the skid marks of the truck, there was the truck itself. The woman's kerchief fluttered in the bramble, struggling to evolve into a bird or a butterfly. Everyone had gone, even the pigs. He had been left behind. The town was not near. His aunt's house was even farther. She would not wait once he had failed to be on the bus. He would have to hitchhike.

Aaron's worry subsided. These were hospitable people, and he was, after all, reasonably respectable in his jacket and gray slacks, even if he wasn't wearing a tie.

He started down the road, too pleased with the countryside, the crisp cool air, the deepening shadows just to stand still. After two bends in the road a car came. He held out his thumb. The car slowed, then picked up speed and passed him by. Another car soon followed, but this one not only didn't slow down, it also honked its horn as it sped by. The next car ignored him completely. He should have waited near the overturned truck. A man in distress would not be left alone in his misfortune. Another car passed. Two teenagers in the front seat and a young girl in the backseat had actually laughed at his plight. He would go back to the truck and make his plea from there.

He turned and saw the pig. It was less than ten feet behind him. It looked at him, then lowered its head and began snouting the pavement. A lone man would have been given a ride, but not a man with a pig.

Aaron stamped his foot. The pig continued its sniffings. Aaron repeated the cry he'd made earlier, but, as before, the pig was unimpressed. A car went by, then another right behind it. Aaron rushed at the pig but had to stop so he wouldn't crash into its lowered head. "Get away! Go! Go away! *Suuee! Suuee! Suuee!* Go home!"

The pig lifted its head slightly and stared at Aaron's shoes, then lowered the snout and rubbed it against a rock in the wall. Aaron stamped his foot again, but got no response. He turned and began again his walk along the side of the road. A car was coming around the bend. He started to raise his arm. He would no longer use his thumb. He would wave his arms, a signal of distress. The car would have to stop. It didn't. The pig, of course, was still following.

There was a repetition of the stamping, stomping, and shouting, but to no effect. "Go on up the hill. You wanted to go up the hill, then go up the hill. Go on. No one's stopping you." Then, again, the stamping, the stomping, the shouting. He was ignored.

Aaron continued toward the town. Cars went by, a truck, a pickup, more cars. He made no attempt to ask for help. He never turned around. He knew he was being followed. There was nothing he could do. And so, as the sun descended and the lengthened shadows spread themselves over the land and the sea, over the islands and the pastures high and low, Aaron walked the darkening road, finally entering the town, arriving at the place chosen for the enactment of his sorrow and his grief, in, it would seem, the custody of a pig.

2

Aaron looked out the bedroom window. There, in the morning light, was the wide pasture that stretched from the house to the headland, smaller than he remembered—which was to be expected since he himself had, in the intervening years, grown to such a formidable height. It had been mowed for hay, the grass short now but too soft to be considered stubble. To him it still seemed forbidden territory and filled, therefore, with unending allure. For fear that he'd go running right off the cliff, or, while playing, chase a ball over the edge, he'd been warned of its dangers and threatened with punishments too fearful to name if he ventured unaccompanied into its precincts. Aware, in her wisdom, that common sense or a concern for his safety and well-being were insufficient proscriptions, Great-Aunt Molly had invented gaping maws hidden in the ground that could open at the touch of his toe and deliver him to an underworld where there were devices designed solely for the enlightenment of disobedient boys. That they involved saucer-eyed creatures of insatiable appetite was hinted at. There, beneath the field, was the haven to which the driven snakes had retreated at Patrick's command, and no appeal to the heavenly saint would be heard above the howls of the regretful children now being introduced to the rites and rituals their defiance had earned for them. (When Aunt Molly had presented this information, it had the form and sound of a plea more than a prohibition. He must, for her sake if not for his own, preserve himself from such a fate. It would torment his aunt to know that, at this moment, he was being, as she put it, "processed." What "processed" meant, she would not say. And, in pity for her, he must never find out.)

Looking out now at the forbidden field, Aaron wondered if he might be allowed at last to walk its length and look down from the headland height onto the beach and the water below. Or, rather, he wondered if he could allow himself to push through the grass unaccompanied by his great aunt, long dead. With his hand in hers, no harm could come. That is what he had been told and that is what he believed. Nor was his belief without foundation. Many times, wide eyed but thrilled, he'd been escorted through the pasture grass, alert to any rumblings beneath his feet, then allowed to sit on the edge of the cliff, his bare feet dangling down, Aunt Molly at his side, sitting too, her shoes and stockings off, both of them wiggling their toes, an insolent offering to the sea, a gesture of scorn directed at the dark forces frustrated by the presence of his aunt and the hold of her hand.

Once, after an excursion made eventful only by their sharing an apple while sitting on the cliff—his great aunt not hesitating to take bites far larger than his—he informed himself that the dangers were nonexistent, that he was being denied pleasures that were his for the taking, that his aunt was unduly frightened on his behalf and he must, casually and perhaps humming a small tune, stroll through the high grass, up to his chest, look out to sea for at least the count of three, then swagger back unharmed and uncaptured, to the vegetable patch he was supposed to be weeding. His aunt would be grateful and relieved by the assurances that he would later give her, allowing her to share in the triumph of his survival.

Not more than four strides had he taken into the forbidden acres when there had been a distinct shudder in the earth beneath his feet. His hummed tune pitched itself into a quick cry of penitence. He twisted his body around and flung himself into the grass that had closed behind him, covering the path he had taken. With another cry he sprang up and, arms held out from his sides as if pleading for the gift of flight, he plunged his way out of the high grass and, stumbling, arms flailing, made his way back to the turnips and parsnips that had been committed to his care. No more would he brave the secret pasture; never again would he experiment in wickedness, nor would he question received truth or doubt imparted mysteries. (That the trembling had come from his own limbs and the low sound from his own bowels failed to occur to him then and did not occur to him now.)

As Aaron looked out the window, a land-borne breeze caught the turf and began an orderly march—small wave upon small wave of bending grass—to the edge of the cliff, flattening one stretch of green, then another, the pale underside exposed to the morning sun before the grass was returned to an upright stand. Then came another breeze, another wave, one after the other, as if the pasture in its pride were mimicking the sea, intimating that it too had depths and stirrings of its own.

Today, Aaron decided, he would begin to grieve in earnest. He would walk the lonely beach, mocked by gulls, uncaring, his every step a stately rebuke to the malign forces that had blighted his fate. His was the tragedy of a man who couldn't have his own way, and he intended to make known his anguish in the solemn solitude that only a stretch of sand, a suspiring sea, and a beetling cliff could provide. He had intended to awaken earlier and make his initial appearance before the sun had fully risen, but his exhausted state combined with the five-hour time difference between home and here had kept him in bed long past the determined hour. And besides, the evening before had not been an easy time for him.

He'd arrived at his aunt's house well after dark. A ruggedly handsome no-nonsense young man with a tawny well-trimmed beard—his name was Sweeney—who had come into town in a small truck, the equivalent of an American pickup, had agreed to take him and the pig the few miles out of town that Aaron had still to go. Some thought had been given to abandoning the pig in the town, but Aaron figured that by now he had labored too hard and endured too much not to be rewarded—no money, of course, just a simple heartfelt thank-you—from the woman with the surprised laugh and the darting eyes. There would be a quiet warmth to her gratitude, a small smile in recognition of the trouble Aaron had taken to deliver the pig safely to its rightful owner. "The least she can do is give us a ham and a few chops, maybe a bit of bacon when the slaughter's done," his aunt had said after he'd explained the pig's presence at his side. But Aaron wanted nothing but a brief rite of abject thanks from a woman overwhelmed to the point of inarticulation by the selflessness of this man who waved away all promise of reward both in this world and the next. And so the pig, with a minimum of encouragement—the threat of a slap from Sweeney—had clattered up the ramp improvised from a door conveniently discovered in the bed of the truck and was carted off to the house of Kitty McCloud after a brief pause at the bus stop outside Dockery's, the pub where Aaron's bags, relieved only of his Walkman and his tapes of Mozart, Bach, and Chopin's Funeral Sonata, were waiting for him.

When he'd knocked on the door of his aunt's house—he'd forgotten that doorbells had long since come to Ireland—a voice had called, "Come in, then! I'm in the kitchen, can't you see?"

Aaron lifted the latch and pushed on the door. It wouldn't open. "It's locked!" he yelled.

"Of course, it's locked. So come around the side, I—no, never mind. I'm on my way."

His aunt opened the door. The room inside was dark and she, too, was standing in the dark. "Aunt Kitty? It's Aaron. I was delayed."

"Delayed? I thought you were coming tomorrow. I'm papering the kitchen so you won't have to see the same old roses from when you were here before."

"Oh. I thought I was coming today."

Sweeney was standing stiff and erect two paces behind Aaron. "Where shall I put the pig?"

"You brought me a pig?" His aunt's voice, surprised, was bright with anticipation and delight. "Now that was a kind thing. And expensive, too. Is it dead or alive? There's my freezer in the basement, so it doesn't really matter. Come in. Come in. Aren't you ever the Greek, bearing gifts." She stepped aside, deeper into the dark. Aaron could see a pale yellow light coming from the kitchen into the hallway that led to the back of the house, but the light was too far away to make of his aunt more than a shadow even darker than the room behind her.

For one swift moment, Aaron thought that the problem of the pig had been resolved—in his favor. He and his aunt would have ham and bacon and chops forever. But he had told Sweeney everything, even before the ride, about the escaped pigs, the run up the hill, the woman with the kerchief. And Sweeney had acknowledged that he had heard the whole story already. Everyone had. And he had written down for him—with a ballpoint pen on a supermarket receipt—the woman's name, known to the whole

town for her independent life, wanting to raise pigs when all of
Ireland had long since given over their pigs to Intensive, the Irish
equivalent of American feed-lot farming, with few actual pig people left. Getting her phone number would be no problem. She'd
come and collect the pig, but small thanks must he expect. The
woman was not noted for her sense of obligation. Aaron had
opened his mouth, ready to defend the woman against such
defamation. The woman had been so cheerful. She knew how to
enjoy calamity, an excellent thing in woman. But he'd said nothing. He was a stranger, a foreigner, and a show of superior knowledge would hardly be welcomed his first night in the town. He
would, no doubt, meet Sweeney again and could put the record
straight after a week or so had passed and his authority as a sage
established. Until then he'd withhold his corrections. And besides, it was the man's pickup and Aaron was tired. Still, if he
gave his aunt the pig, Sweeney could talk. The town would know
him for a thief. The woman would make her claim, and his aunt
would be annoyed.

"It's not my pig," Aaron said. "It belongs to Lolly"—he
turned to Sweeney. "What's her name?"

"McKeever. Lolly McKeever."

The shadow of his aunt seemed to stiffen, if a shadow can be
said to stiffen, raising itself to an even greater height, the women
being taller than he'd expected. (Now that he, Aaron, was grown
and had passed six feet, it was presumed that his aunt would have
diminished. But she hadn't. She, too, had grown. But no matter.
There was the pig to take care of.) "Lolly McKeever's pig, then,"
his aunt said. "Well, that's interesting, isn't it? Lolly McKeever.
And you've brought into the household her very own pig."

Aaron told her the story: the bus, the pigs, the passengers, the
run up the hill and down, the walk to town, the kindness of Mr.
Sweeney. At the sound of the name, his aunt's shadow lengthened

another half a foot. She leaned forward and seemed to be looking over Aaron's shoulder. "So it's you, is it?" she said.

"It is I," Sweeney said. "And it wasn't here I knew I'd be coming until I'd already taken on the pig. And here I am to deliver it. And be gone."

"Put it in the shed, and mind it doesn't eat any of the implements."

And so the pig was locked into the shed. Aaron offered Sweeney a drink for his trouble, but before the man could make his own protest—a half-raised hand, the shake of his head—his aunt, speaking rather abruptly, claimed that there was nothing to drink in the house. Sweeney, saying no more, got quickly into his truck and drove off, backfiring twice. The pig was protesting in the shed. The smell of exhaust fumes filled Aaron's nostrils. "Oh, Sweeney, shut up," his aunt had muttered.

"Sweeney's the man's name, not the pig's," Aaron said.

"All pigs are named Sweeney, a name come down from the Romans. *Sus, suis*. Then the Italians. *Suino*. Then the Irish, the final refinement, into Sweeney. Shame on you for not knowing it. Next time you see the man you might tell him. And tell him who told you. Now, do you want to come into the house?"

Because he could think of no alternative, Aaron had said yes.

They went in the side door, directly into the kitchen, where scrolls of wallpaper, paste pots, and a ladder took up most of the space, including the five chairs and the heavy wooden table. Now he could see his aunt, and she could see him. She was the first to speak. "You've grown no more than that?"

"I'm over six feet."

"Well, you don't look it. Now give me a squeeze, and we'll be the way we used to be and no years between."

He gave her the hug but didn't quite feel the renewal she'd predicted. Still, it was a start, and he was, if not satisfied, at least encouraged by this renewal of family bonds. Standing away after the embrace, Aaron had his first impression confirmed: his aunt was taller than he'd expected. But her lips were still a little too full, her mouth a little too large, and the all-seeing eyes seemed still to find both amusement and disdain in what they saw. The freckles had not faded from her cheekbones or her nose, although her forehead seemed to have cleared. "We'll have fine times again," she was saying. "I can see to that."

Aaron wondered if now was the time to tell her the truth—that he had come here to suffer. He had come to deepen the lines on his forehead, to implant a mournfulness into his eyes that would forever silence the joyful and inspire shame in the indifferent.

Aaron decided he'd wait and tell his aunt another time. Or, better, she would become aware and ask hesitant questions, becoming more sympathetic and compassionate with each and every answer he'd quietly, stoically give. She would be moved. She would admire him. He would become choked with gratitude. Soon, but not now.

Kitty had cleared a space on the table, then on the stove, brushing the wallpaper off to the floor where it could unroll if it wanted to, putting the paste pot on a rear burner so she could use the front. The talk was of Aaron's pig adventure, the young woman's interesting attributes, and the kindness of young Mr. Sweeney. At the mention of the name, his aunt had said, "Maybe you'd like to stop talking and eat what's been put before you." For his first meal in Ireland, Aaron was given spaghetti with enough made for the two of them and the pig besides, with the pig to get most of the tomato sauce. The pig would also enjoy a full box of corn flakes, a near-full jar of applesauce, and what looked like the remains of a tuna fish casserole. (A stalk of celery and a turnip were considered, but decided against. The barley soup and the chocolate pudding, she said, would be saved for the morning.)

The food was stirred into a wholesome mash in a dishpan. Kitty stuck her finger in, then licked it clean. "Let it never be said the guest of a McCloud goes hungry." She stuck her finger in again, licked it again, and nodded her head in approval of what she had wrought. Then she took it out to the pig.

Aaron was given an apple for dessert and told to take it upstairs to his room so she could finish the wallpapering without him in the way. That he had been offered no television, no drink in the living room, surprised him. He had looked forward to refusing. He had wanted to speak of his weariness, to hint at his need for solitude, but he was given no chance. No different from days long gone, he felt be was being shooed up to bed; he'd been enough trouble for one day.

Aaron had dressed by the open window so the ocean breeze could air first his body, then his clothes, cooled by a wind made newly fresh by the pasture dew and the mist not yet fully dissolved out over the sea. He took in a deep breath to fill his lungs with longing, but before he could exhale he saw the pig bound out from the side of the house, more a gamboling lamb than a low-bellied swine. Without pause it trotted into the field and began to root with its snout, digging down into the grass, tearing deep into the turf.

Aaron exhaled. No doubt his aunt had let the pig out of the shed. But its presence, its inclusion in the view, seemed an affront to the sad thoughts he'd begun to generate in his mind. The austerity of the scene was disrupted; no longer was it the perfect setting for the drama he was determined to enact. The cadenced fall of the waves was reduced to distant commentary by the snortings and snufflings that Aaron could hear as clearly as if the pig were there with him in the room. The pig was an intruder, as much on Aaron's sensibilities as on the general scene, and it must be dispatched without delay.

He put on his high thick-soled boots, his Timberlands, presumably waterproof, for walking on the beach. The woman—Lolly whatever-her-name-was—must come and collect the animal immediately. Aaron would even forgo the thanks he'd hoped to receive. The woman could take her good cheer and her pig and move on. He no longer required her gratitude, the surprised smile, the leaping laugh at the sight of the wayward pig returned. The handshake, the soft and healthy grip of her hand in his, the beaming disbelief with which she would greet the tale of his pursuit, the astonished awe she would feel at his proved ability to discipline a renegade—all this he would deny himself. Even the touch of her free hand on his upper arm during the handshake, and the feel of the tip of her shoe against the toe of his boot, all his due reward he would surrender without complaint. Praise for his—and here Aaron stopped in mid-thought. He tied his shoes. The phrase "animal husbandry" had come into his mind. Uncomfortable with its kinky connotations, he blocked further consideration of Lolly what's-her-name's effusions and started downstairs.

The snores coming from his aunt's room as he passed down the hall—at first he thought he was still being pursued by the sounds of the pig—told him that she was not yet up and, by a process of logic that took some few seconds to complete, he deduced that she was not the one who had set free the pig. He went down the stairs and into the kitchen. The room was orderly and immaculate. The wallpapering was done, a pattern of small red roses looking somewhat like diseased bees covering not only the four walls but the ceiling as well. He expected to hear the hum and buzz of the bees' distress. If he were to move he would be attacked, he would be stung, mortally. They would swarm all over him, moving in busy anger over his head, his face, his hands, his entire body.

That the effect of Kitty's labors was so disturbing detracted not at all from the immensity of the task performed. Nor did it take Aaron long to realize his aunt's intent, conscious or subconscious. On the table was a computer, complete with screen and keyboard, with modem and mouse. It was here in the kitchen she did her writing. To protect her solitude she had made the room as inhospitable as she could. No one would pause within these walls. An intruder was dared to intrude. The unease, the discomfort, would discourage anyone this side of insensible. This hive was her domain, the sickly bees her protector and her guard.

Kitty wrote novels of some popularity. Her method, admitted to Aaron alone, was simple. She would take some work that had already proved its appeal and then, as she put it, make her "corrections" and market the book as her own, which, in truth, it would be. Happy endings would be imposed, the proud debased, the humble given the victory. The couplings would be rearranged; one weapon would be substituted for another, hair colors changed and coiffures traded one for the other. Clothing she redistributed with little alteration, the fashions not always surviving, but a chic provided by way of recompense. Gender change solved more than one problem, with new possibilities often suggested. To place the settings beyond the reach of plagiarism, she would mix up the backdrops, the furniture, and the props, creating not so much confusion as, more often than not, an environment the reader found compelling in its singularity and invention.

When Aaron, in a letter responding to her confession, asked why—when she had so much imagination at her disposal, so much craft at her service—why she didn't simply write novels of her own devising, she answered that she was helpless without the anger and frustration aroused by those who'd written the originals. They'd gotten it all wrong, and she would set it right. Their mistakes fueled her imagination; they generated energy. Without the goad of their errors, she had no will, no need to proceed. Her sense of superiority allowed her to see their world and all its people with a clarity made possible by being seen from so great and grand a height, a vision obviously unavailable to her precursors because they had failed to be, quite simply, Kitty McCloud. She was doing them all a favor. She was doing the readers a favor. Taking to herself the burdens of error, she made the necessary revisions. It was not, she claimed, a difficult task. So egregious, so obvious had been their mistakes, that it took minimum effort to return intelligent understanding to its rightful place, to restore the reign of common sense and, in the process, strike a significant blow for the cause of Kitty's bank account. Not with onions and cabbages did she support her acreage, not with parsnips and radishes did she make secure her view of the Western Sea. Her "corrections" had improved upon her inheritance, keeping available to Aaron the stretch of beach below on which he would soon exercise his anguish.

For all the repugnance Aaron felt at the sight of the wallpaper, he couldn't move toward the outside door without pausing to note the book, open at page 276, next to his aunt's computer. He lifted it and read the spine. It was *Jane Eyre*. He put the book down, open at the same page. He remembered a recent letter from his aunt. This was the book currently being "corrected." In Kitty's version it would be the Rochester character, not the madwoman, who would jump from the tower, stricken as he was by Jane's refusal to participate in his proposed bigamy. The novel would end with Jane's cure of the madwoman through kindness and sisterly care, their affectionate friendship, and the fulfillment they would find in the practice of weaving and—again the phrase—animal husbandry. Aaron glanced quickly at the blank computer screen, wished it luck, and continued out the door.

It surprised Aaron that the slam of the screen door, the quick clap, the low thrum, didn't bring on some Proustian recall of his boyhood summers there, an assault of high-clouded days, of rabbits and clams and apples with worms, of bare feet and cow pies and thistles, and of thundering storms with jagged lightning piercing again and again the tortured breast of the sea.

But then he quickly remembered: In his childhood there had been no screen door. This American artifact was introduced into Ireland by his aunt when she returned from her college days at Fordham in the Bronx and realized there was no real reason why the flies had to be invited into the family kitchen. In deference to its newfound Irish identity, she referred to it as a mesh door, allowing the Americans to keep their own designation.

(She also brought back an intensified nationalism inspired by her homesick yearning for County Kerry and, finally—with the exception of a BA in moral theology—a recipe for meat loaf and Apple Brown Betty, a farewell present from a roommate, June Gately, who had majored in economics.)

But now all thoughts of Proust and mesh doors were brought to a fast halt by the devastation he saw spread out before him. His aunt's vegetable garden had been rooted up entirely. The pig's search for grubs and forage had destroyed what Aaron recognized by their remains as tomatoes and cucumbers, peppers and green beans, red cabbage, carrots, leeks and the obligatory potatoes. A patch of herbs—basil, mint, cilantro, and cumin—was now made mulch. Four tall sunflowers that had marked the far boundary of the garden lay facedown in the tumbled earth.

Aaron next saw the shed where the pig had been put for the night. The door hung by its hasp like an appendage connected by a single thread. The hinges had been butted free and the door-frame splintered. Only the padlock had held, keeping the door tipped on its side, resting on a wheelbarrow just to the left of the doorway. Aaron let his eyes shift to the pasture. There the pig was continuing its search, rooting with its snout into the lush green grass, overturning with an efficiency a plow might envy one clump after another, convinced that there was a grub *somewhere* and that finding it would bring rewards beyond measure, beyond price. Snorts and grunts of anticipation accompanied each attempt, and Aaron had to marvel, even in his dismay, at the ability of so blunt an instrument as a pig snout to shovel into the earth and turn it upside down. Without paws or claws it could burrow better than a fox or a rabbit. Without blade or tusk it could dig up a field better than any pitchfork or spade. Bred over the millennia to overfeed and fatten, its instincts for plunder had obviously evolved into a talent for devastation that only the elements of earth, fire, water, and air (and humankind itself) could surpass.

Aaron's first impulse was to go back inside the house, close the screen door quietly behind him, move silently through the kitchen, back up the stairs, into his room, and into the bed, where he would wait to hear his aunt's howls when she would either look out the window or step outside the door. Then, sleepy eyed, he could innocently ask what was the matter. And follow his aunt's directions as to what might or what should be done.

But his annoyance with the pig overwhelmed such wisdom, and he ran into the pasture, once more clapping his hands, once more, as on the hill the day before, shouting, *"Suuueee! Suuueee!"* What this was supposed to accomplish he had no idea. Maybe if he could just stop the animal from further devastation, that would be enough. But there was no place to drive the pig, no place to put it.

The scent of the sea wafted into his nose. Without looking up, he knew the water was there, ahead—and the cliff at the pasture's edge. It would not be his fault. He would, on the contrary, have been trying to warn the pig away from the precipice. But the pig had ignored him. Which had seemed, from the beginning of their association, the pig's preference. He would be innocent. He would proffer his regrets to the lady. (He saw himself holding a hat in his hands, a fedora, passing the rim through fingers as if he were reading there in braille the words of condolence.)

But then in his mind's eye he saw the sad face of Lolly Mc-Keever, whose pig it had been. Resignation would be there, and no blame for him. She knew the pig. She knew its wicked ways. It got what it deserved. He would be praised for his efforts. Offers of restitution would be made. Refusals, reassurances would be admiringly spoken.

"Suueee! Suueee!" Aaron continued his advance, with the pig now getting closer to the cliff. But if he was successful, there would be a rotting pig on the beach. It would stink. It would be unsightly. It would take the crows and cormorants months to pick it clean. No one would want to take the trouble to retrieve the bruised meat and the broken soup bones. It would ruin everything. Unlike Jane Eyre, who, in Charlotte Brontë's version, allowed herself, almost literally, to step—without acknowledgment or hesitation—over the broken bones of a dead madwoman and into the somewhat happy ending plotted for her from the book's first page, Aaron could hardly be expected to step over or around a pig carcass during his mournful walks. This disruption of the prescribed cadence could not be permitted. The pig must not be driven off the cliff, or allowed to take the plunge of its own accord.

"Suueee! Suueee!" Dew from the grass was soaking through the leather of his waterproof boots, but he continued on. *"Suueee! Suueee!"*

The pig, as if weary of this repetition, stopped its rooting, looked once out toward the sea, sniffed the air with its upraised snout, then turned and began to amble back toward what remained of the vegetable patch.

Where he was driving the pig, Aaron had not the least idea. Perhaps this attempt to save the pasture was enough, to save the pig from the lure of the cliff and the call of the sea. *"Suueee! Suueee!"* His cries now were more an admonition than an encouragement, a way of saying "Bad pig" or "Naughty, naughty," as if he were speaking to an impressionable dog and not to an indifferent beast.

The pig returned to the garden. Aaron thought he should make some show of driving it out, but since there was no produce left to save, he let the animal have its way. Perhaps it would content itself there, finding perhaps a small plot as yet undevastated with a few cowering grubs beneath. That it was welcome to them was Aaron's only thought. He would leave it to forage as best it could until his aunt was up and would know what its morning feed should be – if she would agree to feed it at all after all it had done. She had set aside the leftover barley soup, had found a half-empty box of Weetabix and more corn flakes in the pantry and had mentioned some leftover chicken feed in the basement from the time more than a year ago when she'd wanted some fresh eggs and had brought in a small flock that a fox had finished off before the poor hens had had the chance to eat the first of three sacks she'd bought at great expense.

As for himself, Aaron would have no more traffic with the pig. He renounced all responsibility. He would restore the garden, he would repair the shed. But that would be it. To emphasize his resignation, he would now sit on the step leading to the kitchen door and purposely pay no attention to the pig, do what it might. But before he could turn away and head toward the screen door, he saw that one huge hole had been dug in the garden not far from where the fallen sunflowers lay. He tramped through the stubble, the torn plants, and exposed roots, to see what had excited the beast to such extraordinary labor. The hole went at least three feet down and there, at the bottom, was part of an old scarecrow, the lower pants legs sticking out of the still mounded earth at its head. It had on purple socks and heavy shoes, fairly well dressed for a scarecrow.

Aaron felt some impulse to cover it over and then realized where the impulse had come from. It wasn't a scarecrow. Not with shoes and socks on, not with a visible anklebone and a bulge in the pants leg suggesting a knee. He cleared away more dirt. It was a human skeleton. Buried in the garden of his aunt.

3

Aaron walked slowly along the beach, his hands clasped behind him, one knuckle of his right hand pressing against his tailbone. He'd kept his boots on, and the sound of the pebbles beneath his feet was closer to a rattle than a grind. The waves peaked and collapsed about twenty feet from shore with a self-confidence that bordered on the smug. Clouds the shape and size of continents had risen in the west, but were staying close to the horizon, questioning the wisdom of taking on the open sea. The gulls glided silently, content to let the air do all the work, enjoying their mastery of the sky and the beneficence of the accommodating winds. To his right the sandstone cliff—more rust colored than sandstone red—rose almost to the sky, a fringe of pasture grass peering over the top, giddy in the wind, nervous at the drop between it and the rocks below.

A huge stone slab the size of a city bus blocked Aaron's path. It had obviously lost its grip on the cliff and had slid down, unbroken, to the less precarious life on the shores of the sea. It brought to Aaron's mind his aunt's mention in a letter of a few years ago that she was increasingly certain that sooner or later the family land, or a part of it, would probably be tumbled into the sea. No further reference was made in subsequent letters except a parenthetical aside that she was considering the sale of the property while there was still enough of it left to assure an appreciable profit. Her plan was to sell it to some unsuspecting Englishman— some "subject of the Crown," as she invariably put it—and a lawyer for British Petroleum had been mentioned with undisguised glee two years before, but that had been the last he'd heard on the subject.

But now the rock was there to remind him that the advance of the sea was a reality, slow no doubt and without threat for the moment, but a timely goad for his aunt to renew, perhaps, her sweet solicitations of one or the other of Her Majesty's subjects before the acreage was further diminished in so rude and savage a fashion.

At the moment, however, a decision not his aunt's but his own was being forced upon him. He could either squeeze between the rock and the cliff or take off his boots, still wet from the morning grass, wade into the surf, and make his way around the stone from there. He could, of course, climb up and climb down, but he preferred not to break the rhythm of his walk with unexpected excursions. Then, too, he could just turn back. He decided to keep his boots on but take the water route anyway. He wouldn't even bother to roll up his pants legs. The stately pace must not be interrupted. If he got wet, he'd get dry. Discomfort he would accept as a mere change of condition, denying it the power to distress or disturb. And once past the boulder, he would take up his meditation of the lost Phila Rambeaux.

The water fussed at his ankles, then at his shins, then at his knees. There was more of an undertow than he'd expected, and he had to put his hand on the stone to steady himself as he went. When, just before he'd made the turn at the far side of the rock, the water rose to his crotch, cold and, for whatever reason, wetter than he'd expected, he considered going back. Maybe that would be best.

But he had made it to the far side and was safely back on the beach. He'd go on. The water now came right up to the foot of the cliff, lapping against the rock face itself. The tide was in. Soon it would go out. The beach would reappear. He would continue his walk.

As a concession to the tide he took off his boots and his socks after all, stuffed the socks into the shoes, tied the shoelaces together with a slip knot and hung the shoes over his shoulder. His pants legs he rolled to the knee. Thus prepared, he trudged on, the pebbles a pleasant and varied pressure against the soles of his bare feet, the tide respecting the waterline he'd set at the rolled cuff of his pants leg.

Now he would think of Phila. But other thoughts blocked his way. His aunt had not called the police. With the pig occupied in the pasture, they had, he and his aunt together, uncovered the rest of the skeleton. Aaron was allowed to use a spade from the shed for only the first few feet; their hands must do the rest so no damage would be done to what remained of the man lying there. Slowly the earth was scooped away, his aunt's hands moving in an uninterrupted flow, one handful after another, as if she were clearing away water rather than earth. When Aaron was digging too quickly, his aunt's hand touched his arm, an indication that he should proceed more reverently. They were not rescuing the man. There was no need to hurry. (Even at that, they had, without consultation, cleared first the face, the head, then the rest of the body.)

It was not a gruesome sight. No flesh remained, only patches of what seemed like parchment stuck onto the cheekbones and jaw as if the man had nicked himself shaving and had applied bits of toilet paper to stop the bleeding. The earth-stained bones were brown, but the teeth, once Kitty had brushed the tips of her fingers along them, were a shining white, still planted firmly into the jawbone, a perfect row, a classic dental demonstration of what flossing

and fluoride could do. With less care she wiped the forehead and
the sides of the skull, not bothering to clear the eye sockets or dis-
lodge the dirt from the nostrils. But when they came to the hands,
she took the bones into her own hand, one by one, and gently
scraped sway the earth, picking in among the knuckles, rubbing
the tips of the fingers along the palm of her hand, as close to a man-
icure as she could get, given that the fingernails themselves had
disappeared. For a moment it seemed that she was going to press
the hand to her lips, but she simply held it, staring at it, then
placed it again at the man's side where it had lain for so long.

Whenever she came to a grub or wormlike creature working
its way through the earth or along one of the bones, in and
through the clothes, she would pick it up and drop it on the
mound growing at the side of the hole. A flat stone, a shard of hard
sharp flint, lay in the chest and next to the skull was a round rock
like a misplaced pillow. These his aunt rubbed and scraped until
they were cleaned, as if they too were skeletal parts deserving of
care. She then placed them, the round one on top of the flat, at the
head of the grave. Other stones were added, two taken from the
crook of the left arm, one from the pelvis, two from the right
thigh, others from the folds and wrinkles of the worm-tattered
clothes. By the time they'd uncovered the body, she had built a
small cairn marking at last where the man had lain.

There was a baseball cap on the head, and he was wearing
what must have been his Sunday best, a suit of dark wool. Navy
blue it seemed, the purple socks and the impressive shoes, the
heels well worn. His shirt, shredded now into strips, could have
been white, possibly even starched, the rim of the collar still
jabbed into the jaw. Like a half-eaten nut at his throat, what had
been the knot of a tie held a few wisps of dark silk that reached
down past the first button of the suit coat. Someone had neglected
to tuck it in. The tattered clothes, the holes with the bones show-

ing through, the opened seams suggested that their deterioration was no different under the earth than it would have been above. If the clothing was not in such fine condition, it could be said that this was the natural state arrived at after doing harsh and awful service, the world and the weather having had their way, one moment a rip here, a tear there, a hole appearing now, a slit then, until a Sunday suit had taken to itself the effects of the working day, the unending labors, its payment for the privilege of being worn on a good man's back.

When the body was completely uncovered, Kitty sat back on her haunches and spoke for the first time since she'd instructed Aaron to use his hands instead of the spade. "This is Declan Tovey," she said. "I know him by the cap and the suit and the shoes and the tie. Didn't I sew this button on myself." She reached down and lightly touched the second button on the jacket. It came loose and slipped away, down to the side. "Well, nothing stays forever, does it?" She withdrew her hand and put it on her lap. "We all thought he'd gone off, as usual, to who knows where, and here he's been all this time." Again she reached down, now to lift from his sleeve a lump of dirt. She put it on the mound at her side, then leaned over and took yet another clump from his pants leg, and one from his chest as if she were picking lint, occupying herself as she spoke. "He could build a house with four boards and enough stones for a chimney and make the roof of water reeds cut from the bog not far inland. The last of the last. A troubadour, but with strong hands instead of a song. A journeyman who never stayed but always came back. And then the work would get done where there'd been no man to do it. That shed he built, and now it's Lolly McKeever's pig wrecked it to a ruin. And it's Lolly McKeever put this poor man here, and it's only right Lolly McKeever's pig has dug him up. Put him here she did, so the blame would come to me, that I was the one murdered him. And look at the way she's buried him! Just stretched him out and dumped the dirt on him and only three feet down for a pig to find."

Aaron had kept alert for a pause where he might interject some expression of astonishment or ask a pertinent question, but he soon realized it was a vain hope. The monologue, the soliloquy, the extended speech fueled by a fiery passion was, he knew, an Irish invention, one of the country's more notable contributions to the stultification of the civilized world. The Greeks had merely "anticipated" the form, which had reached its destined fulfillment in, of course, Shakespeare, who, as is generally known, was Irish, his use of the soliloquy the proof of it—if proof of the undeniable was needed.

"Of course he wouldn't stay with her," his aunt was saying. "The scrawny thing, even with all those pigs to make his life worthwhile and keep him busy. And she'd keep him busy all right. The slut. Couldn't bear to let him off of her. Had to have him on her and all over her at every hour of the day and night, and hear him calling out her name and sucking every last bit of her flesh into his lovely mouth, no matter where the flesh might be. He'd search it out and take it to himself. Like a beast, then tender as a babe. And must he go? And couldn't he stay? And didn't every last thing she had belong to him? Just so he'd come back to her and cover her over with himself and his hands and his mouth and the crush of his chest and the hold of his arms and the tickle of his toes along her skin and the great heave of himself mining for what's known to be beyond the price of gold. But he wouldn't stay, not him. Had to go. Her time was up. Onto his back, slung across his shoulder, the black bag with the tools and the socks and the warm sweater and the cap that's on him now. And nothing for her but the need of him. And so what could she do but bring him down with a hit on the head, the greedy slut with her slavering all over him and her moanings day and night."

Aaron wanted to keep his aunt from saying more, but there was no stopping her. Now she was cleaning the dirt from the cheekbones and the forehead, forcing the skull to move from side to side. "No farther than the door would she let him go, and she bashed him on the head. And he's dead on the floor. So what can she do but bring him here and put him where the cabbages were going to grow. And look at him now, without even a sheet to cover him over, the stingy slut, she was that pissed off at him."

Kitty had taken up the left hand and was picking the dirt from the joints, blowing on the bones with quick breaths to make sure the job was properly done. "Well, we can't let him here like this, not in the state he's in. It's hardly a decent grave if every pig that comes along is going to snout its way into his crotch. Come on. I'm going to need your help." She let the hand fall onto the thighbone and stood up. When Aaron got up from where he'd been kneeling, his foot knocked against a cabbage and sent it rolling down into the grave, onto the crotch recently mentioned by his aunt.

"Bring the cabbage," she said somewhat mournfully. "It'll do for lunch." She headed toward the house. The screen door slammed.

Aaron knelt down again and leaned into the grave to retrieve the cabbage. The earth beneath his knees began to give way. He braced himself against the mound of dirt but couldn't figure out how to stand up without sliding down on top of the bones. As he pondered, the earth itself decided to continue its shift. He went facedown onto the cabbage, his knees touching the dead man's shoes. A worm was feasting on a cabbage leaf. Aaron slid his left arm out and put the hand next to Declan Tovey's elbow. The right hand he put next to the man's other elbow and, in effect, he began doing pushups, which at least took his nose out of the cabbage and away from the worm.

He heard the screen door slam again. Now his aunt was at the side of the grave. "What are you doing now? Whatever is it? You *are* the peculiar one, aren't you? Well, stop it and get up and come help."

Aaron rested his forehead on the cabbage, slackened his arms, and thought he'd rest a minute before making another try. His knees were on Tovey's shinbones, the skeletal fingers touching his thighs. The worm had left its leaf and was crawling along the side of Aaron's nose. He brushed it away, but it clung to his fingertip. He wiped the finger against the dead man's coat, just below the shoulder. The cloth parted at his touch, a readymade hole into which the worm might crawl.

"Get up from there. This is nothing for anyone to see, whatever it is."

"I slipped."

"I can't hear you. Stop muttering, and get up and get out of there."

Aaron did as he was told, with his aunt's help. He'd had to shove aside the one leg, and if it hadn't been for the strong hold of his aunt's hand, he would have slipped back down and probably broken the shinbone where his knee had been resting. "I slipped," he repeated.

"Please. Spare me."

"Well, I did."

"Mm-hmm."

Kitty had in her other hand what looked like a folded tablecloth with strewn daffodils for its design. But when she flung it open, billowing it out in front of her, he saw that it was a bedsheet generous in size and brilliant in its yellows and greens, a field of flowers one would like very much to lie down on. Aaron assumed his aunt would cover the body with the sheet so it wouldn't be exposed while they waited for the *gardaí*, for the police. But such was not the case.

First his aunt, with no difficulty, removed the cabbage from the grave and placed it at the foot of the cairn. Then, with some maneuvering, with a shifting of the corpse, turning the bones toward him, then toward herself, pulling and shoving and tugging the sheet, a sling was spread under the skeleton. With his aunt on one side and himself on the other, the two of them, at the count of three, stood up (without incident) and raised the bones, the skull now resting on the chest, one hand completely detached from an arm, the cap shoved low on the forehead, the left pants leg raised up above the purple sock showing the white bone that his pants had protected from the dirt. They took him inside the house and laid him out on the bed in what was called "the priest's room," downstairs, across the hall from the kitchen. This was the room that Aaron, as a child, had never been allowed to enter. He'd had to sneak in, which he did, but not too often. It was called the priest's room to honor the legend that the house had been built long years ago to hide fugitive priests in flight from the English. There had also been talk of a secret passage, a tunnel really, under the house that led to the beach where a boat would be waiting. Quite naturally, Aaron, as boy-in-residence, had searched and searched again for the passageway, not only in the house itself but at the foot of the cliffs, behind rocks and in the smallest cove. But he had never found it. If the tunnel was sealed, if the earth had reclaimed it and filled it in and the entrances long since stopped up, he would, in a way, have been happy for the reassurance. His reasoning had been that if the tunnel led from the house to the sea, it could also lead from the sea to the house. Creatures of the deep, modeled mostly after not just Grendel but Grendel's mother as well, had more than once been heard in that boyhood time slowly scraping their way toward him in his bed, the scaly flesh brushing against the tunnel walls, making sounds like the heavy breath of a hungry slug. If, in his boyhood days, he had lost his faith, it was restored in those moments. He prayed, he pleaded, he promised. And, to prove that his beliefs were not contingent upon such emergencies, he often held fast to his faith until well past lunch the next day, whereupon, with a full stomach and a slaked thirst, he would again assert his scorn for superstition, his independence of hierarchical edict, and a brave defiance of deific concern. His apostasy would sustain him rather handsomely until the next time Grendel made his scaly way through the priestly catacombs, having caught the scent of a rebellious and infidel boy.

The room itself was aptly furnished. The bed was narrow, the mattress thin, the covers—mostly a faded patchwork quilt—spare. Only the pillow at the head made concession to some need for a last comfort before the journey might begin—or end.

There was, instead of a dresser, a small cabinet with a single drawer. The cabinet had once held a mirror, and the supports, curved, with a crossbar, looked now like an unstrung harp, its song long silenced, the strains taken up by the winds that carried it to the chimneys of the towns around. A spindle-backed chair, with one spindle a lighter color than the rest, stood near the cabinet, and, along the wall opposite the bed was a wooden bench, not unlike a pew dedicated to discomfort, almost Protestant in its severity. On its back someone had carved the letter *I*, and part of what might have become the letter *H*, if the artisan had not been interrupted in his task and hauled off to the gallows. There was a small table with legs so thin and feeble that it would seem daring, if not foolish, to put so much on it as the rough linen scarf that was there at the moment, both clean and crisp. Aaron had, at the time of the great aunt's telling, a fear more than a doubt that this very table was, in fact, the altar upon which the desperate priest would celebrate his mass, the rickety legs supporting not only the

book and the candles but the goblet of wine and the wafer of bread
along with the crucifix still balanced near the table's edge.

The window was shuttered, to be opened only on those days the
room was given its ritual airing, but closed at all other times since
it was never known when a knock at the door might announce the
outlaw priest's arrival, with the sudden closing of the shutters a signal to those in pursuit. Then, too, so the closed shutters might not
advertise the presence of a priest, and the open shutters his absence,
they were simply closed eternally, and any who saw them in their
unchanging state might surmise what they wished.

The skeleton of Declan Tovey was placed on the bed. Some of the
bones were, by now, disconnected and mixed up, but once the sheet
had been spread open on the bed, his aunt, as if reorganizing the
place settings on a dinner table, managed to put him back together
in a reasonable likeness of what the man had been when they'd first
dug him up. The baseball cap—the word "Brewers" now visible—
was placed farther back so that the visor wouldn't shade his forehead. Then the hands were placed on the chest in typical
laying-out fashion, then put at his sides. Finally one hand—the
right—was put on the chest and the other allowed to rest casually
on the hipbone. The last remaining button on the jacket had come
loose and had slipped down onto the sheet transforming one of the
daffodils into a black-eyed Susan. His aunt made no effort to put it
back in place, as though allowing nature to take its course.

The main difficulty was with the feet. They kept flopping, each
one to the side in imitation of a ballet dancer in first position. When
the tips of the shoes were leaned one against the other, it made the
man look pigeon-toed.

"Go get some pillows from the couch," Kitty said. "We'll prop
the feet. We can't have him looking silly."

"Aren't the police going to say something because we moved the body?"

"What police?" She tried crossing the ankles, but the feet still flopped sideways.

"The *gardaí*. When you call them. When they come to——"

"Who's calling the *gardaí*?" First position was tried again, but it was not to her satisfaction. "Go get the pillows. And let them be matching. The blue ones, I think, with the green stripes. A bit somber, but then why not?"

"You aren't going to call the *gardaí*?"

"Why would I do a thing like that?"

"The man was murdered."

"The slut." She held the shoes clamped together in her hands so they wouldn't repeat their stubborn insistence on lying on their sides.

Aaron smoothed the sheet up near the pillow. "The police are going to have to be told."

"Told what?"

"That, well, that there's this body——"

"They'll be told nothing of the kind."

"But——"

She let the feet flop. "And have them come and go carting him off?"

"But this is evidence, for starters."

"This is Declan Tovey. And I won't hear him reduced to 'evidence.'"

"A crime bas been committed."

"The slut."

"You—we—we're culpable if we——"

"Nothing wrong with a little culpable here and there. And do I go get the pillows or do you?"

"I'll go."

"The blue ones."

Aaron moved around the bed, past his aunt, and squeezed between the cabinet and the footboard. At the door he stopped but didn't turn around. "Then this woman—Lolly—she gets away with murder?"

"Oh, no. I'll see to her."

He turned toward her. "What does that mean?"

"It means what it says."

"What do you plan to do?"

"That's for me to know and you to find out." She was alternately holding the feet, then letting them go, watching them flop, testing to see if they'd land in the same position each time. After Aaron had seen this repeated three times, he went for the pillows.

The living room was large but with a low ceiling so the heat wouldn't rise too far above one's head. On the north wall was the stone fireplace, the varying colors, rusts, blacks, and browns, suggesting the design of a calico cat. Black soot coated the insides, with wisps of gray rising up the chimney, the old soot burned again to an even more refined ash. Andirons shaped like the bishops from a serious outsize chess set held stretched between them a single log, the birch bark still evident at the ends, the middle burned almost through, a bridge destined to collapse at any moment. The windows, two of them, looked out on a stretch of weed. Beyond that was the road, then the pasture that began the rise to the hill that helped block what winds might come down from the east.

The couch, covered in gray corduroy, looked like a large mud pie, its filling made up of splayed books, a coffee mug, a plate with the remains of a fried egg—the fork stuck up between two of the hefty cushions—a *Vogue* magazine and a *New York Review of Books*, the *Vogue* more dog-eared than the *New York Review*. The coffee table was a sturdy construction of pine planks stained the color of walnut, and anchored by four fat legs that seemed the remains of four fat rolling pins. On top of the table was a clutter of CDs, one with a picture of Bach wearing what looked like a dyed-red wig. A heavy brown knit sweater was wadded underneath a single shoe with no shoelaces. There was a stack of books about to topple, the *Irish Times* (disheveled and with a column on the front page torn away), a white porcelain bowl with what looked like a single peach pit placed perfectly in the center, the TV remote, and a brass candlestick holding not a candle but a bulb of garlic.

Aaron picked up the blue cushion crammed against the arm of the couch and looked for its mate. It was under the armchair, along with another plate, this one completely clean except for a hardened swirl of something green. He picked up the cushion. On one side was a stain the same shade of green as on the plate. Aaron guessed it was, in both instances, pesto.

Before going through the door, back to the hall, back to the priest's room, he noticed, to his left, the bookshelves lining the entire wall from floor to ceiling, the spines of the books fading, the lettering dim. Here were the complete works of Jane Austen and George Eliot, the writings of the Brontë sisters, all three, and Thomas Hardy to keep them company. These were the sources and inspirations for the highly successful novels his aunt "relieved herself of"—as one critic noted—"with a regularity most people reserve for another function."

The voice of his aunt intruded. "I'm waiting for the cushions. Have you fallen down the well, then?"

Aaron felt the need to stall. "I'm looking for the second one." He went back and sat down on the armchair, hugging the pillows to his chest. His aunt had murdered her lover. So vivid had been her descriptions of the other woman's needs, so emphatic her feelings of betrayal, so heated her speech, Aaron had little doubt that it could be only of herself that she had been speaking. It was she who'd struck the deadly blow and sent the man sprawled out onto the floor. It was she who'd buried him in the garden. Aaron wasn't sure if she intended to keep the remains in the priest's room—available for visitations—or return him to the ground at a more respectable depth. What was he to do? After Aaron had pondered the question for a full two minutes and come up with no answers, he called out, "I found it," and took the cushions into the priest's room.

Aunt Kitty had lowered her forehead onto the tips of Declan Tovey's shoes, the shoes themselves still clamped between her hands. Aaron waited, but she didn't move. "I found it. The other cushion. Here." He spoke quietly.

"Put them then where they belong, one alongside each foot so he's not disgraced by a foolish posture."

Aaron did as he was told, slightly rolling each cushion so it would hold more firmly the helpless feet. His aunt had not yet raised her head.

"Is there more I can do?"

"Call Lolly McKeever and tell her to come and pick up her pig." Still she didn't move, her hands still holding the feet clasped between her hands, her forehead still resting on the tips of the shoes.

"Call her now?" Aaron asked.

"Now." Kitty's voice was low.

A single gull was careening high over Aaron's head, the wings flicking almost imperceptibly to accommodate the shifting winds coming in from the sea. Now the wings were flapping, desperately it seemed, as if all support had suddenly vanished and only this frantic effort would keep the bird from dropping down into the water below. It disappeared over the top of the cliff, but now Aaron could hear its screech and scream, scolding the elements for their sudden treachery. The water had risen to above the roll of his pants leg. The tide was not going out. It was coming in. Aaron, with a sigh, turned and started walking back toward the switch-back path that zigzagged up the cliff. The water was cold, cold enough to numb his feet if he didn't move faster than he was moving now. He moved faster.

The sea itself was quiet, the waves no more than a series of slight swellings, too low to crest and fall and froth. They simply flattened themselves out and made their small contribution to the tide that now reached above Aaron's knees. There were no waves battering the cliffs to Aaron's left, no thrown spume to lash his face and sting his eyes. There was merely the sly and teasing rise of the water, imperceptible in its inchings, taking its measure from those body parts newly soaked: below the knee, the knee, above the knee, the lower thigh. Aaron looked to see if some watermark on the cliff would let him know how high the tide might come. The line was clear enough. The water had stained the stones to the height of Aaron's nose.

By now he was slogging. The water was mid-thigh and it took considerable effort to force one leg ahead of the other and keep him moving along what had been the beach. He had no memory of the tide coming this far, of claiming all the available land at the foot of the cliffs. To his left was a small cave he hadn't seen before, with a stone the size of a football about to loosen itself from the rounded roof and fall with a merry splash into the rising tide. A fossilized artifact? The lost toy of a Druid child, unearthed at last? Aaron had no time for speculation. And his energies should be rationed out to his legs, not given to the synapses chattering foolishly in his brain.

And yet it seemed right that his mind should search for distractions. The effort it took to move one leg, then another, was replicate of a dream, the slow, effortful push, the impeded movement, the inability of the limbs to make progress no matter how desperate the urgings. He raised his arms from his sides, partly to keep his designer watch from getting wet but also to promote some mutation of his arms into wings, as he had tried to do as a child. If only nature would consider it a possibility, if only the evolutionary process could be speeded up on his behalf, he would be mightily grateful. Often enough in dreams he had flown. It required no more than a mild expenditure of the will, a spiritual lifting, the easy employment of a competence he kept forgetting he had.

He slogged on, the freezing water threatening the warm blood of his dick, his balls, the water forcing a retreat of the waiting sperm, leaving behind a shrunken flap of flesh and a shriveled nut, the two appendages threatening in their deprivation and their shame to disappear completely.

Beneath his feet the pebbles became more pointed, and even the growing numbness of his soles provided no protection against the pokes and jabs of the sharpened stones. The common assumption that the water would smooth them, that the washing sea would lubricate the surfaces for easier passage, proved false. The stones were no longer the beach; they belonged now to the sea. They were resentful; they were annoyed and they wanted this land-born, mud-dwelling intruder to feel the full force of their petulance. Aaron was certain that the soles of his feet were bleeding from a thousand cuts, that he was making a sizable contribution to the crimson tide.

Possible rescue appeared ahead—the huge table of stone that had fallen from the cliff and had blocked his path. It seemed both a taunt and a challenge. The water was rising to his waist. Soon his circulation would stop. Strength he still had, and energy, but the rock was at least a hundred yards away. He wondered if he should strip, if the lightened load would provide the difference between making it to the rock and not making it. He decided, by some circuitous reasoning unavailable to his conscious mind, to give up his belt. The rest of his clothes he'd continue to wear—for the time being at least. If they got too heavy, he'd shed them along the way.

He slid into the water. His boots, still slung by the shoestrings over his shoulder, floated away toward the sea. His watch's claim to be waterproof was now being tested—severely. With each stroke of his arm, with each plunge of his hand, he seemed to douse it again and again, angry now that he had made it a cause for concern, that he had been so prissy in his protection. His purpose, as he swam closer and closer to the rock, was to punish his watch. He had no other intent. Take that! And that! And that! Given so strong a goad, he quickly gained the rock.

He climbed on top. Had he given up his clothes, his skin might have been too slippery, but the coarse cotton of his denim shirt and the strong weave of his khakis clung nicely to the sandstone surface. With a minimum of clawing and scratching he got himself up out of the water and sprawled and spread-eagled himself on the cold surface. He'd stay still for a few moments, surrender to the rock, too exhausted for any act beyond relief—and, of course, a quick look at his watch. The second hand was still sweeping its way around the face. The big hand was between the seven and the eight, the small hand was close to the three. It was, he deduced, about twenty to three Irish time. He closed his eyes. He kept them closed to the count of three, then opened them. He took two more breaths, deep, taking in the salt smell of the rock that made him think of summers past. He must stop indulging himself. He had not washed ashore, saved from a sunken ship. He'd had a simple swim. That and nothing more. He had no right to his exhaustion. He was an excellent swimmer, or at least had been. He'd even been awarded a plaque more than several years before, attesting to his successful swim off the Long Island shore.

What he had done now was negligible. He'd got wet; he'd got cold. Now he would get dry; now he would get warm. And the swim, if he'd only pause to take note, had excited his energies instead of depleting them. He paused, took note, and sat up.

Some distance off, two men in a fishing boat waved at him then returned their attention to the other side of the boat. No gulls flew overhead, but a lone crow circled high above, laughing its raucous laugh at Aaron's plight. The water no longer seemed to be rising, but the sea swells were beginning to crest, to fall, to send their froth rising toward the rock, disappointed that they could not reach the tips of his toes.

The time had come to meditate on Phila Rambeaux, to sit solitary on this rock, fasten his gaze seaward, and brood on loss and the impossibilities of love. He would recall her face, her gesture when, in his class, she would rub her thigh with the heel of her left hand as if trying to erase something she had written on her green plaid skirt. Or the way she would, with her index finger, place her hair back behind her ear, forgetting that the hair was too short to stay there for more than the second it took her to take her finger away. Or maybe he would opt for the abstract, for a general melancholy that would give his sorrows a more universal cast, his woe identified with the woe of the world. Until now he had been unfaithful to Phila. Almost a full day gone and he'd given her almost no thought at all. No pangs had pierced, no yearnings had struggled to find release, to wander, to search, never to find. The grieving that he owed her had been left unexercised. It was time to make amends.

He looked at his watch. It would now be a quarter to three. He could mourn at least until the water had receded to knee height. How long that might be he did not know, but he didn't require that he should. His grief could easily outlast the ebbing tide. It was eternal. He might even wait for the tide to return, then ebb again before leaving off his meditations. Phila, his beloved, deserved no less.

But then he wouldn't be at his aunt's when Lolly McKeever would come for her pig. He had phoned her. She was due at three. She hadn't sounded particularly eager to make the retrieval nor had she given him thanks for his efforts. His tale of tenacity was cut short before he'd even told her about the top of the hill. The cheerfulness with which she'd responded to the dispersed pigs was apparently reserved for catastrophe and not for rescue. "At three then. And don't feed it until I'm there." With that she had hung up, as if Aaron had been some rash intruder calling to solicit funds for some obscure cause. He had hoped to hear her laugh, but she hadn't laughed at all.

It then occurred to Aaron that this woman might indeed be, as Kitty had claimed, the jealous killer of the man in the garden. It also occurred to him that Kitty might take the opportunity of Lolly's visit to confront her with the remains and force a confession. There would be a spirited exchange of words, of accusations, denials, and, possibly, counteraccusations. Kitty was, to Aaron's mind, as much a candidate for the crime as the woman she'd named. How the scene between the two of them might end Aaron had no notion. But he should be there. He was, after all, a writer. This display of human conflict, of murder and of love, should not pass unseen by the artist's eye. He owed it to himself and to his readers, to those dependent on him for uncommon insights, to say nothing of high drama and the amusement that only a killing can provide.

Sleek as a seal, Aaron slithered from the rock into the water. He'd swim the distance to the switchback path, then walk the road back to the house. He was wet anyway and accustomed by now to the cold. Maybe Lolly McKeever would still be there when he'd arrive, and she would see him soaked and dripping, having just risen, like Cuchulain of old, up out of the sea.

4

T hat's not my pig."

Lolly McKeever stood near the shed looking more at the damaged door than at the pig snuffling its way through the pasture grass between the house and the cliff. She swung the dangling hinge open, then shut, loosening the last screw so that the hinge fell clattering onto the hardened ground that surrounded the shed. "Sorry," she said, then put the tips of her fingers on the door itself as if to complete the damage done by the pig and release the door, letting it, like the hinge, fall at her feet. But the lock held fast and the door swayed only slightly, still secure with one corner dug into the earth, an almost balletic toehold that held it balanced free of all other support except for the sturdy hasp of the padlock that refused to let go.

"What do you mean, it's not your pig?" Kitty picked up the hinge, dusted it off, blew the dirt from its surface, then dropped it again, cleansed, onto the ground.

"It's not my pig."

Kitty gave the hinge a kick. It moved no more than an inch. "Tell her, Aaron," she said.

Aaron, shivering in his wet clothes, had been trying not to let his teeth chatter or his body twitch. The sea, to complete the trouble it had caused him, had sent a stiff breeze from off its vasty deeps, making sure that the brine soaking his shirt and pants sustained the near-arctic temperatures they had enjoyed before they had been sponged up out of their native element and been brought so thoughtlessly to this arrogant headland. The sea had not finished with him yet. Now the drying salt began to sting his flesh and shrink his skin and there was as well the stench of dried seaweed and rotting fish. Only a pelting rain could help him now, cleanse and warm him, but the sky was a pitiless and uncharacteristic blue, and the sun seemed more mockingly benign than it had ever been on these primal shores from the beginning of time. He looked at Lolly McKeever and opened his mouth. Lolly, for the first time, looked at him. Her eyes brightened, her mouth opened, and she let out a laugh of pleasure and delight, similar to the laughter excited by the unmanageable pigs the day before. The sight of Aaron was apparently equal in calamity with the ditched truck and the chaos that followed. Aaron, hurt, confused, moved his jaw up and down, his mouth not quite closing, "I—I—I—I——" He clamped his lips together, swallowed, then tried again. "I —I —I——"

"There, you see?" Kitty said. "The pig was in your herd. As he said, he chased it up the hill and down, and you'd already gone off and left him. And the pig too. But now it's here and you can take it home." Lolly's laughter stopped. She turned her attention from Aaron to the pig. "It's not mine."

"It has to be yours." Kitty had little patience with contradiction.

"It doesn't have to be. And it isn't."

"I'm not going to make you pay damages, if that's what you're so afraid of."

"It's still not my pig."

"How do you know?"

"Just look at it."

"I'm looking at it."

"Well?"

"It looks like your pig and no one else's."

"What a terrible thing to say."

"What's wrong with it?" Kitty took a deep breath and held it. Lolly was being warned. Kitty would hear no words against this pig.

"That low-slung belly, it's not meat, it's not fat. It's just there. What have you been feeding it?"

"I gave it nothing I wouldn't eat myself."

"Poor thing."

"It's a fine and healthy beast and it doesn't need your criticizing."

"I wasn't criticizing. I was evaluating."

"Of course. A pig person like you knows everything."

"I know my own and my own know me."

"Then come and let it have a look at you." Kitty marched toward the pasture. "Come on. We'll see who it recognizes and who it doesn't."

Lolly was looking not toward the pig but toward the cabbage patch. "What's that big hole for in the garden? Is it a swimming pool on its way or what?"

"What hole?"

"That one there."

"A strange thing you should ask, Lolly McKeever."

Lolly shrugged. "Just being neighborly." With that she turned again toward Aaron. She used a small smile to suppress another laugh. "You're the nephew."

Aaron nodded, the movement renewing the shivers he had just managed to control. Lolly McKeever leaned toward him, trying, he supposed, to trace the smell now rising in full force from his shirt and pants. "You fell into the sea." Now the laughter came, greater in its delight than before.

"I—I—I was walking."

"I see." Her eyes became even brighter.

"But I—I had to swim."

"How interesting." The smile forced the laugh to cease. She searched his face, first his eyes, then his lips, then his forehead, his chin, his ears, looking for a clue to his presentation. After she had given the eyes another try, she settled on his right ear and searched no more. "You look nothing like your aunt." And then the laughter came again.

"I—I was born in America." He gave a quick shiver and brought his elbows closer to his sides.

"Ah! Of course." She looked down at his feet. He moved first one foot, then the other, shuffling them in place as if trying to offer some entertainment, some demonstration of their capabilities. With another burst of laughter, Lolly seemed to approve, even applaud the display, to show her gratitude and pleasure at having been treated to this manifestation of his cunning.

If he hadn't been wet, if he weren't shivering and stuttering, he would never have submitted to this scrutiny, this hurtful gaiety, but his psyche had already subscribed to the helplessness of his body, a kind of solidarity, a mutual sympathy he was unable to sever. He surrendered to his imbecilic state and stood quietly before her, his head tilted slightly to the right, a further abjection confirming his idiocy. She could now laugh her eyes right out of her head. He gave her full permission. He looked directly at her. The laughter had ceased.

She was still looking at his bare feet. She seemed thoughtful, even troubled. Aaron considered wiggling his toes, an added performance, an encore to the shuffling he'd already executed for her amusement, but he decided to continue the silent offering of himself and try not to shiver or to twitch. He would also subject the woman to the process of examination she'd been practicing on him.

She had, to begin with, big ears, but she also had a good-size head and the ears didn't look particularly disproportionate. Just big. Capable. No delicacy, no nonsense. He liked that. Ears like hers could listen to anything and not wince. That an ear could wince was a consideration he'd take up another time. For now, Lolly McKeever's ears were quite capable of either wincing or not wincing. She herself would know which response would be right and proper.

Before he could continue his attentions, he began to shiver again, but not from the cold or the wet. Thoughts of Phila Rambeaux, had just passed through him. And in passing they had taken with them his bones, extracting them through his skin, wet as it was, through his salted clothes. His spine was gone and his pelvis too. He might have been left his skull, but the knee sockets had been emptied and all joints released from their joinings and spirited away. He shivered again, trying to hold his body together. Now he was shaking, trembling in every part that Phila had left behind, mostly in his shoulders and his hands.

Lolly McKeever was no longer studying his feet. She was looking at his shoulders, then at his face, just above his right eye. She was neither laughing nor smiling. "Do you drink?"

Before Aaron could deny or affirm, Kitty called from the pasture. "Come see if it recognizes you or not, why don't you?" After a sad shake of her head, Lolly turned and waded into the grass.

Kitty was standing by as the pig snouted up one patch of grass, then another, grunting its disappointment that it had made yet one more faulty choice, taken one more worthless gamble. "It likes it here," Lolly said as she came alongside Kitty. Kitty took one step away not to avoid Lolly but to place the two of them more in front of the pig. "Now let it have a look at you," she said.

The pig shifted, giving the two of them a full view of its hams. To accommodate the move, the women stepped sideways, then began circling the pig from the cliff side of the pasture. Again the pig shifted, again no view was given except its high behind, the skinny legs that ended in what looked like high heels and the corkscrew tail that flicked itself lightly when the turn was completed. The women moved. The pig moved. Again the women moved, this time even closer to the cliff. The pig moved, its adamant hams confronting again the determined women.

More thoughts of Phila Rambeaux passed through Aaron, going in the opposite direction, toward the sea. His bones were returned to him, his joints rejoined, his pelvis and his ribs still aching from the transaction. Now the thoughts were gone. They had deposited the bones in their familiar casing, and they, the bones, must take up again their usual chores. The trembling slowed, then stopped. Aaron moved his jaw and was relieved to discover that he could exercise some control. He might even be able to speak should that requirement ever be made of him again.

Kitty and Lolly, not more than two feet from the edge of the cliff, where the pig had obviously maneuvered them, were appraising the pig's hindquarters, no longer insistent on a full frontal experience. With stiff unsynchronized tilts of the head, a little to the right, a little to the left, like two metronomes— each determined to impose its own beat—the women regarded what they saw with thoughtful interest and skeptical appraisal. Kitty, looking intently at the pig's behind, spoke first. "See? It knows you."

"The hams look like saddlebags. They're too lean."

"Too lean for what?"

"Too lean for it to be my pig."

"You're just being fussy."

"I would hope so."

"Poor darling, look at it. You've made it so ashamed it won't even show its face."

Aaron looked at the pig. It stood motionless except for an intermittent twitching of the ears and a single wiggle of the tail. Its snout seemed to be straining toward Aaron, as if the scent he was giving off was a smell it couldn't quite identify. Again the ears twitched, an encouragement for the women to continue their assessment.

Lolly McKeever turned away and looked out over the water. A breeze lifted her hair lightly, then let it fall back onto her shoulder. She put her hands in the back pockets of her jeans, straining her shirt against her breasts. This could not possibly be for Aaron's benefit. Of that he was sure. Lolly had already dismissed him, and he could think of nothing that might qualify him for reevaluation. The bold presentation of her straining breasts was, he decided, an offering to the sea, a promise to the storm tossed and the shipwrecked that there waited on shore a worthy welcome and an abundant blessing.

Kitty observed Lolly a moment. She pursed her lips and lidded her eyes. "Then you're not taking the pig," she said.

"I take only what's my own."

"Then I'm to keep it."

"For all of me, yes, keep it."

"And I'm to become a swineherd like yourself?"

"If that high you aspire, I can't stop you. And now I have to get back. I'm needed."

"You're going?"

"I'm going." She leaned closer to Kitty. "And is that really your nephew?" She whispered the words.

"Any reason he shouldn't be?"

"Oh, no. No, no. No, no, no." She looked again at Aaron. He shifted from one foot to the other. "Somehow it seems right after all."

The women walked almost warily around the pig, heading toward Lolly's truck. Aaron called out, "Aren't you going to ask her about—you know—what's-his-name. Tovey? Declan Tovey." The women stopped. Neither moved. "I mean,"—Aaron continued—"well, you know what I mean."

Lolly turned toward Kitty. "What *does* he mean?"

"He means Declan," Kitty said. "Have you seen him lately? Declan?"

Her voice was airy, a pretense of nonchalance, a sure sign to Lolly that she was mocking the true gravity of her question.

"Declan Tovey? No. Why would *I* see him?" She started again toward the truck.

"No reason. Except I—I came across him just this morning."

Lolly stopped. "Oh?" She hesitated, then asked, "And how is he these fine days?"

"As well as can be expected."

"Oh? Well, if you see him again, say hello."

"Say hello yourself, why don't you?"

"I will. If I see him."

"You'll see him."

"Maybe. Maybe not."

"You'll see him now. And you can thank my lovely nephew for making it so easy for you."

"Oh?" Lolly raised her head and gazed loftily around, deliberately assuming a blank look. "Strange. I don't see him."

"He's there. In the house. Waiting."

"Oh?"

"Come in, then, and be welcome."

"Another time." She turned again toward Aaron. She seemed about to say something, but after another glance up and down, from his feet to his forehead, words failed her and she made again for the truck.

"Watch you don't fall in the hole," Kitty called. "Since it was you dug it to begin with."

"I?"

"You. If your name is Lolly McKeever, the name of the one who did it to him."

"Did? Did what?"

"Did what was done to him. You."

"I? I?"

"You. Slut."

Lolly drew herself up, the breasts again assuming the prominence displayed for the benefit of all the ships at sea. "I? 'Slut,' you say?"

"Come then and see. I've no patience left."

"I'm needed." Head held not quite as high as before, Lolly turned with some difficulty back toward the truck but seemed reluctant to take a step in its direction.

"He's here."

"And done in?"

"Done."

Aaron looked down at the ground, then decided he'd look out past the cliff. The pig was swinging its body around, no longer needing to keep its face from view. It raised its snout, twitched its ears, and gave yet one more wiggle of its tail. Then it stood there, blinking at the horizon.

As the women tramped toward the kitchen door, Kitty called out to Aaron, "I'm showing her Declan Tovey, if you want to be there to see it."

Lolly McKeever stood on the far side of the bed and looked down at the skeleton that lay stretched out before her. After a pleased guffaw, she slapped her hands onto her chest. "For the sake of Jesus and Mary too!" Then she laughed and put one hand on the shoulder of the skeleton's coat and let it rest there. Kitty had placed herself at the foot of the bed and was holding on to the rail of the wooden footboard. Aaron stepped just inside the door, then moved a little to the side. He liked the way Lolly's hair had fallen forward when she'd bowed her head.

"So here's where Declan Tovey's gone to," Lolly said.

"And you didn't even give him a sheet for a shroud," said Kitty. Lolly looked at Kitty. Kitty looked at Lolly. Lolly shook her head, then took her hand from the skeletal shoulder and touched the top of the cap. "It was you did this thing, and now we know it."

"I?" said Kitty. "Never."

"If never, then never is now. And the reasons are known to all."

"Oh?"

"Declan Tovey was the last of the good stout men, and we all lived to see it. Forget that he was no taller than you see him now; forget that the raven hair was a plume of glory and that the eyes were the eyes of the warrior saint, blazing with a holy light. Forget that his hands could hold your whole face as if it were a chalice and he was about to take a saving drink. Forget that he might lie yourself down to be sacrificed, all writhing around to receive the blessed martyrdom."

Again Aaron's instinct was to interrupt, but the woman was too far gone in soliloquy and had best be left alone. "Forget all that and remember," Lolly continued. "Remember the day he saved the four sons of Maggie Kerwin and the two sons of Sally Fitzgibbon, with their boat going down in the storm sent from the north. Alone in his skiff the man went, hollering. Lost in the waves and found and lost again, with the mountains falling right on top of him. Remember the seething water hissing at his valor, raging that he should defy them all—the waves, the rocks, and all the nibbling fishes below. This was the day he dived down and brought up the four sons of Maggie Kerwin and the two sons of Sally Fitzgibbon, and only him still able to holler. And remember the rescue of Hanrahan's goat with the barn burning, and Kate's cat plucked from the high branches of the oak, and his clothes ripped open for all the world to see. Forget that his words were made of the night air and that he had the gift of transport like none other before him or since, that his closed eyes and open mouth were the surrender of all this world, and that soon enough he'd close his mouth and open his eyes, and all the world was gone away for good. Remember what's there to remember, and forget what's there to be forgot."

Kitty's face had turned from flesh to stone. She took her left hand from the railing and put it on the wooden knob capping the last spindle of the bed frame. After she'd made herself one inch taller, she said, "The four sons drowned and the two sons with them. Hanrahan rescued Hanrahan's goat, and Kate's cat never made it past the roots of the tree."

"Those," said Lolly, "were other times. I spoke only of the days when Declan was there." She paused, then added, "The days that I was with him. And no one else besides."

"And you killed him because he couldn't stand the touch of your hand and had better places to go, transporting or no transporting."

"I?"

"A knock aside the head. One brutal blow." Kitty yanked the cap away, jerking the skull onto the left shoulder. "Look there, where you struck the blow, a crack that could kill any man, even him."

Aaron strained his head higher for a better look but couldn't make out if there was a fracture or not. Lolly touched the skull. "It was you did it," Kitty said. "It was you—and you plowed him into my garden, cracked skull and all."

"I? Plow?"

"You. If your name is McKeever and your father's name before you."

"The plow is your answer. It was Kieran Sweeney, then, who did this thing. It was Kieran Sweeney plowed your garden. My tractor. My plow. But Sweeney was the one, not me, and he put Declan Tovey in where the cabbages would grow."

"Never," said Kitty. "It was this man stretched here did my plowing. Always. In secret he'd do it to please and surprise me. I'd be away and he'd know it. And when I'd come home, all the plowing done."

"It was Sweeney did it."

"Never, I said."

"Always. Ask him."

"I've no words for a Sweeney. Yet I won't hear him accused of deeds he didn't do—plowing or killing or whatever. He had no cause."

"Oh?"

Before his aunt could say anything further, Aaron sneezed. The two women spoke with one voice. "God bless you."

The blessing dispensed, Kitty glared at Lolly. "Tell me the reason," Kitty repeated to Lolly.

Aaron sneezed and again was given the blessing. Lolly smoothed down the cloth strips of what remained of the dead man's shirt. "You know the cause as well as I," she said.

Aaron sneezed once more, the blessing this time taking on the tone of a curse, a warning that his allotment of grace had been exhausted and that further requests for benediction would be either ignored or condemned outright for the selfish and greedy intrusions they were. To distract his body from the need to sneeze, Aaron took up again the shakes and shivers, giving him renewed contact with the wet clothes, coarse with salt and stiffened with their own stench. Bit by bit he was being rubbed raw, and soon there'd be no flesh left. And yet he could hardly leave the room. Lolly McKeever, like his aunt earlier that day, was about to implicate herself further in the murder of Declan Tovey, and she would prove, he was sure, magnificent.

"Jealous. He was jealous."

Lolly said this, then said no more. Both Aaron and Kitty waited. To prime the pump, Kitty finally said, "Jealous?"

Lolly moved the skull back into position and was now tucking the pillow closer to where Declan Tovey's ear had been. "Hmm," she said. She let the back of her hand feel the cheekbone as if testing for a fever.

Kitty, her patience more tried, said, "Jealous. And why jealous? Of what? Of whom? And where?"

Lolly brushed the tips of her fingers along her forehead. "I've said all there is to say."

Kitty took one of her deep breaths, this one into her nose. Aaron was sure it would come back out as smoke and flame. But instead of exhaling, she chose to speak the following: "Kieran Sweeney had no cause and less right to feel jealous about anything that concerns me. And that is the beginning and the end of it all as far as Kieran Sweeney is concerned."

She spoke as a hard fact, but there was a wistful sorrow on her face, in her eyes, and along the wan line of her lips.

Aaron felt cheated. All Lolly McKeever had done was tuck a pillow and feel a cheekbone. His aunt, in turn, had given some substance for the case against Sweeney—his forbidden courtship of her, her forbidden longing for its success—but she had hardly cleared herself of all suspicion. Something there was between her and Tovey, of that there could be no doubt. And something between Tovey and Lolly. But now no one would speak. He could ask questions. But he was not at all sure he would want what answer might be given. He tried to shiver, to retreat back to a time before these latest complications had asserted themselves, but the best he could do was jerk his head and twitch his arms.

"You can keep silent for as long as you like, but it won't change the truth of what I've said." Kitty's tone managed to be both airy and severe at the same time.

Lolly kept her eyes on the hand that was holding the sheet. "Don't you have some better cloth than this for the poor man? He *is* dead, you know." She let go of the sheet, and Declan Tovey's hand slipped onto his groin.

"I know he's dead," said Kitty. "And now it's known who killed him."

Lolly moved the hand farther up onto his stomach, nearer the man's waist, then reached over and brought the other arm up to restore the symmetry unfailingly imposed upon the dead. It gave him the gesture of a man satisfied by a good meal. "Kieran Sweeney," Lolly said, "was driven mad. Let that be said in his defense." The time had come for another of the woman's Irish monologues, and she proceeded with all the eloquence at her considerable command. "The very idea that Declan Tovey would set his eyes on me sent him to a frenzy. And when he saw that the man was allowed into my house to perform intimate acts like scraping my drains and patching my walls where the rot came through, sense left him and his jaw was set. The very notion that the words of this man should slip their way into my ears, that the sight of him should sink in through my eyes, sent him daft. And when Tovey confessed the truth about how he was feeling, about his striving for me alone, about his plans for glory, Sweeney went mad all over himself. Free liquor he gave him, and poor man, Declan that is, that was, his head on the table far past all protest, and what does he do but do him in? When Declan's head is bending low and he's slurring my name with his liquefied tongue, in goes the poison and the drink is drunk. To whose health Declan drank only Kieran can tell us, but down again goes Declan's head on the table, the glass toppled and the dregs running out, and the arms gone limp for good. He's done in. He's dead. And that is when he, when Kieran Sweeney, up and plowed your garden, Kitty Mc-Cloud. Digs up your ground. And in goes Declan Tovey for all time until today. Now let the deed be known, and Sweeney can stop going to church and doing other sanctified acts not fit for a saint."

Three times Lolly had changed the position of Declan's arms, first crossing them on the chest, then moving them back down so the fingers were approaching the crotch, then back to the stomach where they'd started. "Dear Declan," she said, touching the peak of his cap, "I could have saved you, I suppose. I could have denied to Sweeney all the things you said, and only I was supposed to hear. I could have let someone else patch my walls and mend my roof. I could have given to others what was rightly yours, but forgive me if I couldn't, as much as they wanted it and as much as they kept pleading for it. Even to save you from this I couldn't do it, and you've got to forgive me now because I'm asking for it, for to be forgiven." She took her fingers from the top of the cap and put them to her lips, then to her cheek, then let them slide down her chest, something of a secular sign of the cross. When the fingers got to her waist, she hooked them inside her belt buckle and let them stay. Kitty had tilted her head as she gazed, blank eyed, at Lolly, as if only from an odd angle could she properly view the woman as she spoke. Slowly Kitty straightened her head. No emotion showed on her face. It seemed to have shed all muscular responses, to have found a repose so absolutely natural that Aaron barely recognized it as the face of his aunt. The intelligence was gone from the eyes, the amusement from the lips, and the stubbornness from the chin. The nose seemed uninterested in whatever smells the world might offer; the cheeks had completely forgotten whatever laughter they might have known. She was staring at the space above the headboard where an oval picture must once have hung, an egg-shaped pattern of pale yellow put into relief by the surrounding brown. Aaron tried to remember what painting had been there before, but nothing suggested itself. What he could see now might be a work of art itself, the perfect oval, the evocation of an egg unencumbered by the actual picture of an egg, a presentation of "eggness" that had taken genius to devise and years to achieve. Because it lacked detail, because it offered no specific of the actual, it could be studied endlessly, an action to which his aunt seemed to have dedicated herself for the length and breadth of Lolly's speech. Without disrupting her enthrallment, she said, somewhat tonelessly, a voice made level by the depth of her artistic involvement, "So it was with poison you did it. A coward's way, if you ask me. A sneaky way and I'm surprised at you because you're my best and closest friend I ever had. Because what you've done is confess to the crime if ever a confession was made. To think I gave you credit for a hit on the head, a good bold blow, out in the open, so he could see it coming and gasp a prayer or two. You disappoint me, Lolly, after all these years."

If, at that moment, Aaron had been told to make the judgment as to who had committed the crime, he would have been lost completely. Each had stated her case—and one for Sweeney as well—and each had named the means by which the deed was done: a blow to the head (his aunt) or poison (Lolly McKeever). Kieran Sweeney remained a candidate for either method. Forensics would tell. With this thought Aaron arrived at what he considered a Solomonic moment. He would become insistent that the skeleton be put in custody of the *gardaí*. Whichever of the women objected would be the guilty party. Opposition would be an open admission of murder.

"The police, the *gardai*," Aaron said, "they're the ones can tell how it was done and who did it."

"The *gardai*!"

Kitty and Lolly had screeched in unison, each equally aghast at the proposal. And it was in chorus that they said, "Have you taken leave of yourself?" Because Kitty seemed the more choked of the two—but only slightly—it was Lolly who made the first solo effort. "Why would anyone go to the *gardai*?"

Kitty, recovered somewhat, added, "What has this to do with them, of all people?"

"The man was killed," said Aaron.

"And don't we——"

"Know it. And don't——"

"You know it too?"

"What can they tell——"

"Us we don't——"

"Already know?"

The women looked at each other, nodded in unison, then looked at Aaron, more with bewilderment than accusation. Without taking her eyes from Aaron's face, Lolly said to Kitty, "He's your nephew. You be the one talk to him."

Kitty cleared her throat, preparing no doubt for a lengthy speech that would trace the history of Irish jurisprudence and, bringing to bear the Jesuit instincts congenital to the Irish, offer irrefutable proof that in crimes of this kind the usual procedures must be dispensed with and the course of justice channeled not through the corridors of power but allowed a more domestic passage. It was at the hearth rather than at the bench that the truth would be revealed, just as proofs were to be found not in the fluorescent glare of the laboratory but in the flickering light of the fire, the shadows dancing on the faces of the just and the unjust

alike. Truth would be more valued than vengeance, the truth in itself the highest form of punishment. What greater penalty could
be inflicted than that one be known in truth and all one's deeds
cast before the accuser's eye? Unprotected by prison walls, forever
susceptible to the all-knowing gaze of this piercing knowledge,
what contortions of mind and spirit must the guilty devise,
whether in the direction of a cringe or the assumption of an arrogant indifference? Were Lolly the murderer, what worse punishment than to have it known by his aunt? Were his aunt the killer,
what higher vengeance could be exacted than Lolly's knowing
stare and sly smile? Pleas for imprisonment would rend the air,
surrender and public confession would be considered a mercy at
its most necessary. Self-exile would become an option; the se-
cluded life, a comforting consideration. Sackcloth would be a
benevolent cover, and ashes a welcome benediction.

Kitty by now had cleared her throat—twice. The moment
had come and she would speak. "Keep your nose out of this," is
what she said. And that was all she said. Lolly nodded in agree-
ment, her lips pursed with approval. Aaron considered saying,
"But"—but of what might follow he had no notion, so he said
nothing. He simply looked from Kitty to Lolly and back to Kitty
again, then down at Declan, silenced, disarmed by their stares, casual on the surface, defiant at their depths. He must comply. To
persist would bring not their opposition but their dismissal. To
save himself from relegation to the irrelevant, he kept his peace
and continued to look, as if for some show of support, at the man
on the bed. Declan could offer nothing more than a slightly
amused grin made more self-satisfied by the absence of a limiting
mouth that would have circumscribed the bared teeth seen now in
one unmitigated leer.

Aaron's ploy about summoning the *gardaí* had accomplished
nothing beyond further befuddlement. The two women were

equal in their disdain. He believed both, in turn, to be guilty. Since this was an impossibility, be began to have stirrings in the back of his brain that a third person (Sweeney) might be the culprit.

He now heard Kitty say to Lolly. "Do you want the pig or do you not want the pig?"

In what seemed a somewhat strange answer Lolly cried out, "Quick! Close the door. Quick! The door! You—whatever your name is—quick, before he sees in."

"Aaron," Aaron said. "We were introduced."

"Aaron, please, the—oh, my God, he's looking into the hole, there in the garden." Kitty, looking out through the screen door on the far side of the kitchen, was wringing her hands, something Aaron was certain she had never done in her entire life. "Don't— don't let him look in. Don't——"

Aaron moved away from the wall and looked past the kitchen and out the door, into the garden. Kieran Sweeney, from the night before and recently mentioned in this very room, was bent over the open grave, staring down into it. Sweeney looked closer, then stood up and moved nearer the cairn. Aaron doubted the man could see through the screen door into the kitchen, much less through the hall and into the room where they were gathered. Before Aaron could decide what to do, Lolly came from her side of the bed, brushed past Kitty and grabbed Aaron by the arm. She swung him slightly to his right so that he was facing the hall directly. She then gave him a shove and slammed the door behind him. It was his instinct to turn around, knock on the door, and ask that he be readmitted, but before he could make his move, he heard Kitty's voice through the door. "Get rid of him. Get him out of here." There was a pause, then Lolly added, "And don't let him see in here. Whatever you do, don't open this door. Do you understand?" Aaron nodded. "Can you hear me?" Lolly asked. Aaron started to nod again, then said, "Yeah."

By now Sweeney was kneeling at the foot of the grave. He was bending forward, scraping against the earth just beneath where he was kneeling. The pig had come to watch. Sweeney seemed to have found something that encouraged him to dig more rapidly. He was tugging at what looked, from the distance, like a rope. There was resistance and he pulled harder, then scraped away more earth. He was tugging, trying desperately to pull something free of the dirt. More earth was removed, and the tugging, now a prolonged straining, was resumed. All the man's muscles, all his thoughts and feelings, seemed to be given over to pulling on the rope. The pig continued to watch.

Finally what looked like a sack came loose, the earth gave way, and Sweeney was tumbled into the grave, disappearing completely. Aaron went through the kitchen, past the table and the sink, to the screen door. Sweeney's head appeared, then an arm. He was sitting like a man in a bathtub. He started to get up, but something was in the way. He reached down, pulled up a good-size sack, made of leather—or earth-stiffened cloth—then flung it out onto the mound of earth next to the grave. Aaron heard a rattling, then a clunk. The pig's hind leg had been grazed, but the pig didn't seem to mind. Sweeney looked around, surveying his situation. He placed his hands, palms down, next to the sack, stiffened his arms and tried to hoist himself up. He had lifted himself about six inches when the ground under his hands crumbled and his face was sent full force into the dirt. For a moment he didn't move, letting his face rest where it had landed, his arms at his sides, himself kneeling inside the hole. The pig heaved itself away from the kneeling figure and trotted toward the tool shed.

Sweeney lifted his head, shook it, wiped his forehead, brushed his sleeve across his eyes and mouth, spit, and stood up. He flicked the dirt from his sweater, from his pants, giving special attention to his knees. He then lifted one foot, knocking away what chunks of earth were there, then lifted the other foot, repeating the act. He hiked up his pants, spit once more and moved his sleeve across his mouth.

Aaron could withhold his help no longer. He stepped into the side yard, letting the screen door slam so that Lolly and his aunt would know he'd gone outside. "Mr. Sweeney," he called, managing not to sound too alarmed by the man's difficulty. "Mr. Mc-Cloud" was Sweeney's reply, surprised and cheerful, as if he hadn't expected to see him and was pleased at his good fortune. Before Aaron could offer his assistance, Sweeney said, "And what happened to you? You're wet to the bone."

Aaron's clothes felt the wet all over again; the salt rubbed itself more meanly into his skin. The sea smell, the stink of fish, however, seemed to have diminished, but that could be because he was catching cold and his nose was being rendered inoperative.

"The tide came in," Aaron said.

Sweeney, still cheerful, said, "You'll catch your death." Aaron, on cue, sneezed. "Bless you. Bless you."

"Thanks."

"You were walking on the beach?" Sweeney seemed troubled by the vision he'd conjured up.

"Yes."

"Far down the beach, to the north?"

"Yes."

"Below the headland where it's all rock?"

"Yes."

"And then the tide came in?"

"Yes."

Sweeney's solemnity increased as the inquiry progressed. He

had put one hand on each side of the grave and stood like an interrogator totally unaware that he was down in a hole. "And the water rose?"

"Yes. The water rose."

"To the cliffs it came, to the foot of the cliff, and then it began to climb? The water? To climb?"

"Yes." Aaron sneezed but received no blessing.

"And you'd nowhere to go but out to sea?"

"There was a rock."

"The rock. Yes, the rock. You climbed the rock. And just in time. It's what I've been warning for years. Years." By now his solemnity was absolute.

"Are the tides rising higher and higher?" Aaron asked.

"Oh, no, not that. It's anyone could know that, if he's any sense at all. It's that we don't do the fishing as much as we used to. The fishings have gone underfoot. All gone." Squarely the man stood like someone in a pulpit, sending forth his knowledge and wisdom not from a height but from a depth. And he seemed most pleased with the inversion. "No one drowns anymore," he said. "There hasn't been a drowning in three years. Before, we could count on ten to a season at the least. But not enough go fishing, not enough get claimed by the sea. And after all these years, the sea hasn't got used to it. It's developed an appetite. It's looking, the sea is, the sea's looking for someone—anyone will do—someone to drown. And it's going to keep rising and rising and coming farther inland and farther until it gets its due. It'll eat away the cliffs and even bring the rocks down onto itself, into its very bosom, looking, searching, not leaving until it's found someone to drown. The sea isn't famous for yielding its secrets. But it's after us all. You on your rock, you have to watch out. It's got sight of you and there, look at your clothes, it's made its claim. You smell of it already, so it will know where to find you." He nodded, sure of the truth he'd spoken, his arms stretched out from his sides, taking the measure of Declan Tovey's grave. "Keep your distance from the sea. It's asked for you by name, and I'm ready to bet at any time that it'll get you yet."

"I'm too good a swimmer."

"A good swimmer is the best prize of all."

"I didn't stay on the rock. I swam all the way back to where the path takes you up to the road."

"Good. Good. Give the sea a taste of what lies ahead. Tease it a bit. Swim a little. Walk along the shore. Tease it. Taunt it. And see what it does." He made a noise at the back of his throat as if he were gargling with mud. "Meantime, don't catch cold. That's no way to go when you've already been promised elsewhere."

With what he hoped was a cold dignity, Aaron asked, "Do you need some help?"

In response the man said, "Want to see what I've got here?" He put one hand on the earth-encrusted sack. He smiled a conspirator's smile, his eyes catching a glint from the sun. "You want to know what's inside?"

Aaron shrugged.

"I'll tell you. Do you know a thatcher's tools?

"Thatcher's?"

"A roof thatcher. His tools. They're here, in this sack. A dutchman and a leggett and some tarred twine and I can tell you besides, there's a cup, like a chalice really, all made of purest pewter, for taking a drink. It's in there, too."

"May I look?"

Sweeney put his hand on the sack. "No need to. I just told you."

"Oh." Aaron scratched his collarbone because it seemed the gesture of a stupid man and he wanted to appear stupid, incapable of knowing what the man might be talking about.

"You want some help out of there?"

"What kind of a man is it who can't get himself up out of a hole?" Sweeney, with a little assist from his hands and arms, sprang sideways and was upright on the level ground in less time than it took Aaron to blink. Sweeney was picking up the sack with one hand and brushing off his pants with the other. "I'm home to my cows now, but I'll come back when he's been returned to the ground. To see that he's safely away. Deeper, tell them, much deeper. And give this to your aunt and tell her I understand why she couldn't come out to say a word or two, and Lolly McKeever too." He paused, then said, "You know, of course, she murdered him."

"Who?"

"Declan Tovey."

"You said murdered by someone. Who?"

"Who but her?"

"Who's her?"

"Must I say her name?"

"Lolly McKeever, you mean."

"No, not that one. The other one."

"Are you talking about my aunt?"

"You mustn't blame her. She had cause."

"She says Lolly did it."

"Of course she'd say that. But it's your own aunt who did it. And you've got to accept the truth."

"I don't think I do."

"Of course you don't. Because you didn't know what the woman was going through with this rascal all night and all day and all the times between. Forcing himself on her, insinuating in his insinuating ways. Doing for her all manner of things a man can do and all the time waiting to make his move. And then he makes it. But she'll have none of it. Not she. Not this woman. Into her own hands she takes the leggett, the iron implement from here in the bag, and she warns him. And he's getting closer. And she warns him again and moves off. But he's following and she's warning and gripping the leggett, and he's closer and she's against the wall. She has no choice. Aside the head she gives him the leggett. Not just to send him off, but to get him gone for good. To the floor he falls and she knows she's done it. And no regrets, none at all. He was given nothing he didn't earn. He'll never come after her never again. Never, do you hear? Never!"

Sweeney's eyes were blazing. He had worked his way not to an old wrath but to a triumphant bliss lived all over again. Sweeney had done it. Tovey was after his aunt. Sweeney was jealous. And he had just, in his own way, stated the motive and the means, jealousy and the instrument in the thatcher's bag. Aaron was relieved. He was giddy. Although he rather liked Sweeney. He had, after all, given him a ride, even with a pig. But now his aunt and Lolly were free. He could now convince them to turn the bones over to the *gardaí*. The case could be solved in minutes. Proof of Sweeney's guilt was in the man's hand. The sack. It held the murder weapon. He had come for it. It would have fingerprints. Aaron would testify. The murder was solved.

Sweeney had picked up the sack and held it out to Aaron. "Tell your aunt this comes from me. I was the one found it, but it's on her land and she's the one should have it. But be sure to tell her it's from me, and if she could part with the cup I'd be grateful."

Aaron looked at the sack. Sweeney was undoing all his detection. He was surrendering into the hands of his aunt the probable murder weapon. The proof of his guilt. After two hesitant movements of his hand, Aaron took the sack. "I'll tell her. It's from you." He held the sack at his side. There was no rattle. The clogged earth had muted whatever sounds it might want to make. It wasn't as heavy as Aaron had expected. He gave it a shake to see if he could hear the murder weapon. All he heard was a dull *thunk*.

Sweeney was kneeling again, his head lowered into the hole. He reached down and picked up a pebble, then stood up and showed it to Aaron. "Give this too to your aunt." It was the metal button that had come off Tovey's coat. Sweeney rubbed the dirt off with his thumb and held out the button. Aaron took it. Sweeney smiled again the conspirator's smile. "But I'll still want the pewter cup."

"I'll tell her."

Aaron drew the sack closer to himself, switched it from his right to his left hand and let it rest against his thigh. Getting dirt on his pants was the least of his worries. Sweeney had continued to smile, not moving away from the hole. Aaron realized it was his responsibility to leave first. "Thank you," he said, giving the sack a shove with his knee. "I'll tell my aunt."

Sweeney nodded. "And tell her her secret's safe with me. Not that it wasn't an evil thing to do. But she was provoked, and I honor her for fending off what she'd rather die than do. That much I know, and I credit her for it. She has a name I'll never speak, not even to accuse. You'll tell her that."

Aaron nodded, turned and started toward the house. He knew Sweeney was watching. He walked faster. A new thought came to him. The pewter cup held the traces of poison. Instead of taking the cup, he'd asked for it, sure it would be given. Aaron picked up his pace. Then he slowed. This latest reasoning was inconsistent with the other confessions. The man had said a blow to the head. He should have claimed poison. But he hadn't. Aaron stopped walking altogether. Then it was all clear. Sweeney wanted his aunt to know he'd done it. Jealous of Tovey, maddened with love, he'd poisoned the poor unsuspecting man. And now he wanted full credit from the woman who'd driven him to so rash an act.

Lolly had been right, right in every respect. It had been

Sweeney, and the proof was in his hands. Lolly was free. His aunt was free.

The sack became heavier. Aaron was walking again, his pace accelerating the closer he got to the house. He saw ahead of him his aunt staring out through the screen door. On her face was a stoic sadness. Aaron glanced back over his shoulder. Sweeney was standing, his hands at his sides, his mouth slightly open. He was leaning forward in the direction of the screen door. When Aaron turned again, his aunt abruptly moved back into the kitchen and disappeared. He took a few steps closer. When he looked over his shoulder again he saw Kieran Sweeney on his knees, placing one stone on another, reconstructing with patient fidelity the cairn his aunt had built to mark the grave of Declan Tovey.

5

Aaron was surprised. The pub—Dockery's—appeared to be a quiet place, more murmurous than raucous, a flow of talk interrupted by an occasional laugh, then dropping again to a level suggesting easy but animated discourse. The four tables lined along the wall were of such sturdy but crude construction that they seemed to have come down, generation to generation, from the drinking hall of an ancient chief. The chairs, in contrast, were made of bentwood with dark red leather seats, inherited from a tearoom or a sandwich shop. Two booths in the back seemed improvised from old cabinets, but again the tables were made of wood cut from the forest primeval and built by craftsmen indifferent to design. The tops, brown made black by time, were at least four inches thick, readily able to sustain the carved and scored markings that pitted and pocked their surfaces. The legs were, by contrast, a little spindly, cut it seemed from the staff of some pilgrim who had crossed the mountains long years before, the tables held up more by faith than by physics. The floor was unvarnished wood, raw wide boards better suited to the deck of a trawler than a dining room, shredded and splintered beneath the soles and heels of at least several generations.

It was the bar itself, however, that gave the room its distinction. Of heavy and highly polished walnut, it had the aspect of a high altar in the church of a somewhat prosperous parish, the niches and shelves rising to the height of the room itself, enshrining the bottles and glasses, the ambers and crystals, the opals and emeralds, statuary magnificent and well worthy of the worship they received. The top of the counter gleamed auburn, the reddish tint beneath the brown showing through like a promise that under the surface lay pleasures yet to be revealed. Blue traceries coursed through the white porcelain shafts that brought forth the ales and stouts and beers, the array of handles themselves suggesting a console to be played, an instrument requiring dexterity and stamina, not to be approached by the uninitiated or the ungifted.

There were no bar stools. If you couldn't stand, you should be off and away, a wise policy winnowing the wheat from the chaff, a means of sparing the upright the company of culls. The bartender, Francis—his name the word most often repeated on the premises with the possible exception of "fuck"—was a tall young man, lean and limber, with a wide jaw, a generous but seemly nose, nicely spaced brown eyes, and a proportionate forehead lightly screened by a fall of straight brown hair. To give him some distinction, he had a wide mouth and also a tongue the generous jaw and mouth could not oblige. Constrained by intrusive teeth, the tongue would block the air passing along its sides and give to the speech of handsome Francis a light slur, adding an *h* to an *s*, turning a "yes" into a "yesh." For some this was a defect, for others a lure, and it was widely known that the good man's tongue was, more often than not, given an appreciation that easily compensated for whatever difficulty he might have with diction and enunciation.

Aaron would have preferred a booth along the far wall, but it seemed unfair and unwise to appropriate that much space for himself alone—especially since "alone" was the operative word for the evening. He wanted to be alone. And he was. It had been a difficult day, a day of distractions. His brain had been poked and jabbed and stuffed and turned here and twisted there, what with a skeleton and three possible killers, one of them his kin, one a woman of possible allure, and one a man who seemed to be the sworn enemy of the woman he loved, Aaron's enigmatic aunt.

The man was Aaron's preferred suspect—not just out of a chivalric impulse that would spare the ladies but an informed determination based, no more, no less, on the sure knowledge that one of the other suspects was a member of his family and the other a woman with auburn hair. From being their accuser, he was now promoted to self-appointed protector. So certain was he of his judgment that he'd been tempted, once left alone with the skeleton, to call the *gardaí* and let justice take what course it would.

Kitty had gone off to London to sign a contract for her latest completed effort: a correction of *Oliver Twist* in which Nancy reforms Bill Sykes, they marry and adopt Oliver, after which all three lead vitalizing and challenging lives in lower-class London. Kitty then, in a daring act of cross-fertilization, conspired to have Oliver later marry Little Nell—who, conveniently, failed to die but would, soon enough, in Oliver's arms.

Lolly was making another attempt to get her pigs to market and, like Kitty, would not be available for consultation and decision until late tomorrow. Lolly's last words before driving off were, "Don't go burying the bones till I come back." Kitty, on leaving for the airport, had issued a similar decree, adding, "He'll do all right until I'm home."

Aaron had given himself a few moments alone with Declan bedded down in the priest's room. He would let the skeleton itself tell him what to do: call the *gardaí*, bury him again, or let him enjoy his rest after so frantic a day, what with the arranging and rearranging by the accused and accusing women. When Aaron had stared down at the skull, he'd seen nothing but delight. By the grin Aaron could tell the man was reveling in all the fuss. The last thing he wanted was a quick resolution. This prompted Aaron's resolve to toss him back into his grave with his sack of tools and to cover him over with dirt and cabbages and stones and any other irreverent implement he might find in the vicinity.

But then either the women or the pig would dig him up again. The only solution was the *gardaí*. When Aaron lifted the phone in the kitchen, however, he was reminded that the authorities might not subscribe to his theory of the murder, that Sweeney, for all his preferred guilt, might be innocent and the accusing finger pointed at someone whose protector he now was. He put down the phone. Declan Tovey could enjoy his rest. Aaron would eat the hot dogs his aunt had left in the refrigerator and, possibly, heat up the canned tomato soup she'd pointed to on the pantry shelf. He would feed the pig the pellets from a fifty-pound sack Lolly had donated from the back of her truck. He would shower and clothe himself in the studied casualness best suited to his particular brand of pretension. He would then go down the road to Dockery's and leave behind the distractions that had lured him so far from his set purpose of flaying himself with thoughts of Phila Rambeaux. All the livelong day Phila had been given only scraps and leavings, moments of attention that never managed to lengthen sufficiently to allow for actual suffering. What the beach had not achieved, the bar would surely provide. Here in the crowd he could be all the more solitary—even if the room wasn't all that crowded. He would stand here, at the end of the bar, unnoted, unremarked. He would look at nothing but the mounting bottles and into the few spaces of mirror unblocked by the sacred display.

Since he wanted a long drawn-out descent into the depths, he would drink with measured sips as befits someone pondering his loss, a man who has given himself over to numbering like rosary beads the sorrowful mysteries of his recent life, thoughts that would sustain his sense of injury and nourish his belief that he was beyond all possible succor.

Trapped somewhere in the thin membrane between the conscious and subconscious there was a knowledge that he, Aaron, was obsessed by Phila rather than in love with her. He had chosen her to love him—which, in turn, would save him the trouble of having to love her. And he had been willing to do almost anything he could to achieve her compliance. When she declined the honor—without giving it an even cursory consideration—the rejection provided Aaron with all the elements needed to persuade himself he was in love: jealousy, rage, sorrow, yearning and inconsolable need.

But he wasn't in love. He had, quite simply, been denied what he had wanted, and now the components of thwarted love had been appropriated to himself in support of the tantrum his efforts had earned him. All this Aaron knew and would not deny if he were to force some confrontation between himself and himself. But for the time being he made the usual excuse: Suffering was suffering, no matter what its source, no matter the worthiness or unworthiness of its cause. His anguish was real, and the egotism of its origin was of no account whatsoever. That Aaron had brought his sufferings upon himself was beside the point. The suffering was there. And fool though he may be, he was still a fool who embodied the tenacity of human longing, the ability peculiar to his species, to yearn and yearn again without repose, even when all hope had died.

"Aaron McCloud," Francis said. "You've come back. And looking brilliant." They shook hands. Aaron ordered a pint of Guinness.

After the appropriate time of drawing and resting, Francis set the glass in front of him. Aaron took a fair gulp. The taste, of course, was of sour coffee, a taste he'd come to enjoy, but there was, unavoidably, as always with Guinness, the disappointed expectation. The dark brown liquid had the appearance of root beer and Aaron, try as he might, could never get beyond this early preference.

He took a second gulp. His disappointment lessened and he knew that by the time he had emptied the glass, his maturation from root beer to stout would have been accomplished and he could, with full commitment, order a second pint.

"I hear you got yourself a pig," Francis said.

"Oh. Yeah." Aaron, who was still wondering how Francis had known his name, was even more astonished to realize that his troublesome acquisition had become common knowledge. And if the pig were a known presence, what about Declan Tovey? How could Tovey's bones—of far greater consequence—have escaped the notice of whatever omniscience kept its all-seeing eye trained on local events large and small? Aaron considered posing a few leading questions that might encourage Francis to tell what he knew, but decided that at the first dropped hint, the reporter in Francis would be roused and Aaron would be subjected to an inquisition leading to an inevitable confession that would implicate his aunt and deliver into the hands of the *gardaí* the grinning bones of the felled thatcher. Aaron would keep his mouth shut for a change. And besides, he had come for other purposes than to discuss a renegade pig and the unearthed corpse of a murdered vagabond. He assumed that his self-exile from the other customers would be respected and he could now move on to his assignation with the elusive Phila Rambeaux.

Francis had put both hands on the top of the bar, one on each side of Aaron's glass.

"Lolly McKeever says it isn't hers, but I wouldn't be too quick to believe. An old animal, they say, and Lolly's ashamed. Still, to disown your own pig." He shook his head.

"You want it?" Aaron asked. "It's yours if you say so."

"No. Not me. I work nights, like this [thish], and it wouldn't be fair to the pig."

Aaron decided not to follow the logic of this statement. Instead he took several good gulps of the stout, expecting that Francis, impatient with this suspension of their talk, would move down the bar and converse with those who had no sufferings to indulge, no grievings to enjoy. But as he drank he saw over the rim of his glass, in the mirror behind the bar, the entrance of Lolly McKeever, conjured, it would seem, by the mere mention of her name. A man was with her, taller than Lolly but shorter than Aaron. He was wearing a dark suit, a white shirt with a thin knit tie, and, if Aaron saw right, heavy-soled shoes in want of a shine. His dark hair, slicked back, gave him a look suggesting an inborn potency, a look to which Aaron had long aspired but had yet to achieve. Aaron's impression was reinforced by the gesture the man was making toward a table not far from the door, a casual command, a gesture that could be made only by someone never known to displease or to disappoint. Lolly, without pause, slid into the chair next to the wall, leaned forward and put her elbows on the table.

She was wearing a pair of trim tan slacks and a woolen sweater of Aran origin. She seemed to have cut her hair and, in the intermittent light of the room, it had become darker and more severe. She was less attractive than he remembered, but the man's presence at her side suggested that she was more desirable than he'd thought.

The man chose not the chair next to her but the one opposite. He slouched slightly and put his hands on the table. Lolly was talking. They had been talking when they'd entered, and this seemed a simple continuation, the subject of sufficient interest to sustain itself during the rubric of their arrival and the ordering of their drinks. Now the man leaned forward. Lolly, after a moment, leaned back but without taking her eyes off the man's hands. She cocked her head to the left, skeptical perhaps but more likely an increase of interest. Now Lolly leaned forward. Aaron waited for the man to lean back, but even after Aaron had downed another drawn-out gulp, the man kept his forward position.

Aaron looked down into his glass. The thought that he himself had taken the trouble to make himself presentable for the evening offered some relief. He hadn't intended to get all dressed up, but before he'd realized what he'd done, he had dressed in a stiffly woven white shirt, a pair of pressed khaki pants, and the Alfani shoes that had had the mud cleaned off. He'd combed his hair, then tousled it to give himself a more athletic look. Examining himself in the mirror he'd become convinced that he had been, in these two days in Ireland, transformed from a somewhat drab man now past thirty to someone newly arrived at the fullness of his youth, the eagerness of his early years firmed into manly assurance, the sweet smooth flesh now textured with experience, the hesitant eyes made bold, ready for any condescension that might prove necessary, the lips freshly plumped as if they, like his penis, could swell in anticipation of uses soon to come. His clothes felt tailored, fashioned expertly to accommodate the broad shoulders, the tapering torso, the hard thighs, to say nothing of the slender hips and the resolute buttocks—long seen as vestigial evidence that he was descended from centaurs. The tousled hair, in its well-crafted chaos, provided not only a proper crown but would reassure the onlooker that here was civilization at a moment of true fulfillment: the snakes of the Medusa not only tamed and domesticated but divinely transformed in their writhings into the curls and locks and errant strands that, while tumbling comfortably into one another, still suggested the presence of the primal, the potential reversion to mythic terrors and uncontrollable consequences.

In other words Aaron felt uncommonly preferred, more than ready to be seen by anyone who, like himself, might chance into Dockery's bar on this clear and lovely night.

At least a third of Aaron's pint had yet to be drunk. He took one gulp, then another. Lolly hadn't moved, nor had the man. Aaron tried to study the froth lines tracing the patterns on the side of his glass, but he soon found himself looking again into the mirror, waiting for the next move to be made, Lolly's or the man's, backward or forward, to the left or to the right, with the hands on or off the table, Lolly speaking or Lolly listening.

It annoyed Aaron that he was giving his attention to Lolly McKeever and to the man who was with her. His experience of her earlier that day had certainly been sufficient. Beyond being a potential killer, she was, he told himself, of no interest whatsoever. He should stop looking in the mirror.

After he'd found himself looking two more times, he got up and, with the self-conscious ease of a cowboy who assumes he's being intently watched, his shoulders shifting from side to side, the set gaze focused straight ahead, Aaron did his best to saunter over to the dartboard. He plucked the three red-feathered darts—not feathers, actually, but a Darwinian mutation of plastic called "hard poly"—he pulled them from the cork and went back past the gray painted line measuring the required distance from the board. Set into the space between the bar and the back wall and sufficiently distant from the booths, the game was isolated in its own niche but still visible from almost anywhere in the room, with the player's back to the assembled—except when he would return from retrieving the thrown darts for yet another try. With a not unpracticed ease he threw the first dart. A single 20. He tossed a second. It kissed off the wire and bounced out. The third, a treble 7. Careful not to move too eagerly, he collected the darts. The first toss landed in the narrow rim surrounding the bull's-eye. A single bull. Before he could make his second throw, a man holding his pint came and stood behind him, just to the right. Aaron tried to affect an even greater ease, an indifference he wanted desperately to feel. After a few forward jabs of the held dart he made the toss. A double 9. The man moved closer. Aaron's third toss landed dead center. A double bull.

While retrieving the darts another man came to stand a few feet behind the drawn line. Aaron considered going back to the bar, but the second man was handing him a full pint. "You're the first McCloud to make a single and a double bull in one round," he said. "In all the years, the first."

"Thank you," said Aaron. He accepted the pint, sipped, then set it on the end of the bar next to his other glass, still unemptied.

"Do you mind?" asked the man. He was holding three darts, the yellow hard polys.

"Well," said Aaron, "I haven't played in a long time. A fluke, the single and the double bull."

"All you McClouds are known liars and the better for it. Are you for a quick game?"

"Why not?"

The man was short and squat with a huge head, his neck no more than a crease between his chin and his chest. Only a taut string could have penetrated through to the actual neck bone. He was wheezing slightly, a faint sound of flapping mucus marking each inhalation, each exhalation. He was pink. His face was pink, his hands were pink, his bald head was pink. Aaron had the suspicion they'd met before, then realized that he was thinking of the pig. He knew immediately who would win at whatever game they might decide to play.

The man took the first game, reducing his numbers from the designated 301 to zero by doubling out on the double 17. Aaron still had 132 points left, the object of the game being to erase the given 301 to zero with as few throws as possible. In the second game, Aaron fared better: the man zero, Aaron 93.

Each time Aaron went to retrieve his darts he would, as he returned to his station behind the line, observe the various positions being taken by Lolly and her companion. The variants were few, but he sensed a growing intensity in the conversation. Lolly had begun to keep her hand on her glass, the man to put his arms, not just his hands, on the table, his elbows now six inches from the edge. Neither of them seemed aware of the game.

During the third round a woman—young, blond, wearing a pink T-shirt, tight jeans, and overpriced sneakers—came to watch. Between one of Aaron's throws and the throws of the pig man, she put her initials on the scoreboard—CC—meaning she would like to play the winner. She was holding her own set of darts, the blue polys. The pig man, as pitiless as only one eager for involvement with a beautiful woman can be, played out the game with seven tosses, going out on a double one. Aaron, who would not have minded Lolly seeing him in competition with a young blond, was still stuck with 197.

Justice, however, soon asserted itself. In direct combat with the woman, the pig man was undone. Sweating, twitching, he forgot the needed mathematics, to say nothing of the loss of his well-aimed eye and purposeful toss. The woman went out on a double 3, leaving his opponent, if not in the dust, at least with 199 unerased points.

The pig man, a brave smile in his lips, insisted on buying a round, including a drink for a spectator a little off to the right. The young woman declined the drink and the offer of a match with the spectator. She had to get back to her boyfriend, who was talking to a woman even younger and with hair at least as blond. The spectator accepted the drink, a glass of red wine, which, to Aaron's chagrin, scandalized no one. After the appropriate salutations, the spectator took up the cause of the blue polys, and a new game was begun—one only—between himself and Aaron.

While waiting his turn, Aaron from the side of his eye thought he could see Lolly looking in his direction. He was tempted to turn and make sure, but his opponent had stirred up some excitement in the pig man by scoring 140—two treble 20 and a single 20. Another round of drinks was ordered. The game was mercifully ended with the man's double 9.

Just as Aaron was about to offer the red polyed darts to a man at the end of the bar, a fellow distinguished by his yellow suspenders, he saw Lolly's escort advance in his direction. Aaron hesitated, then made the offer to the suspendered man. The fellow looked down at the darts, puzzled as to what they might be, then accepted, suspicious that he was committing himself to something not quite acceptable in polite society. Aaron stood up to the bar, drained his pint, and nodded to Francis, the equivalent of a spoken request. Francis obliged, whispering, "Nesh time take the yellow. Better balance."

Before Aaron could acknowledge the advice, Francis, to demonstrate his neutrality and disinterest, moved to the far end of the bar and listened to a teenager lecture him on the impropriety of electing a woman to public office. Master bartender that he was, he listened with no response beyond the occasional blink of an eye, the nod of his head, the lift of his chin.

To his left Aaron could see the darts fly by, some in a straight line, others in a high and graceful arc, some in a slight wobble. The pig man had teamed with the spectator against Lolly's friend and the fellow in the yellow suspenders. Aaron could make out the colors—red, blue, yellow, green. From behind him came grunts, chuckles, groans, phrases like "Unlucky" and "Good darts," and silence. Again the darts went past like hummingbirds. He would concentrate on his drink. He would find within himself the waiting grief. He would give Phila her due, a full complement of jealousy and anguish, forcing them to their limits and, if possible, beyond. Now was the time to see how much he could bear, how much he could sustain without losing consciousness; he might at least test to see how far he could go without obliterating his sense of decorum, when the bitter tears would drop, diluting his stout, disturbing the surface pattern that now suggested a fleur-de-lys.

He took a hefty gulp. The pattern changed to roiled waters receding from the rocks. After another gulp he saw the palm lines of a woman's hand, the lifeline long, the love line almost nonexistent. He made a quiet snort through his nose, then gulped again. He put the glass on the bar without checking the pattern and looked instead into the mirror.

Lolly, from her table, was watching the dart game with complete absorption. To see where her escort might be, Aaron shifted first his head, then his feet, to give himself a different angle from which to look into the mirror. There he was, his hair now falling over his forehead, the knot of his tie pulled down, the top button of his shirt unbuttoned. He was aiming a yellow-polyed dart. With a quick flick of the hand he released the dart. His face registered no reaction, no indication of success or failure. Aaron emptied his glass and raised his hand, signaling Francis. When Francis failed to notice, he used the back of the hand to wipe his lips so the gesture wouldn't be wasted.

He looked down into the emptied glass, stuck his finger into it, wiped it along the sides and put the finger into his mouth. He considered repeating the procedure but, in the mirror, he saw Lolly looking at him—or so it seemed at the distance and in the dim light. She had watched him put his finger in his mouth. To assure her it was an acceptable gesture, he did it again, this time making it seem that he was performing a taste test requiring thought and judgment. He let the finger stay longer in his mouth, lowering his eyes as if ruminating. When he checked the mirror again, Lolly had returned her attention to the game.

Francis, upon whom the raised hand had finally registered, put a fresh pint in front of Aaron. To avoid having to interpret any patterns, he took a quick sip, put the glass down on the bar, and, to the sound of a few hands clapping, sauntered even more casually than before toward the dart game. The applause had not been for him. A game had been completed after, it appeared, some rather heated playing. No indication of the victor was given, no handshakes, no forced smiles, no humble shrugs. Lolly was smiling—but at what or at whom he had no idea. But it was clearly a smile of satisfaction, the eyes steady and amused. Some expectation had been fulfilled. Perhaps her friend had won. Or quite possibly she was responding to the sight of Aaron with his finger stuck in his mouth.

Aaron circled the small crowd, avoiding any acknowledgment of Lolly. The game had ended. The original spectator was retiring from the field. "Need anyone for another game?" Aaron asked the pig man.

"You're on," was the immediate reply. "A team, can it be? The two of us? Against the two of them?" The "two of them" consisted of Lolly's friend and the fellow with the suspenders. Aaron nodded. The starting score was set at five hundred one, team match, a double to get in—no point applicable until the player hit a double—and a double to get out—the final throw having to bring the score exactly to the winning zero. Best of three.

The first game began. Aaron was the last to qualify, but finally by aiming at the double 20 he hit a double 3, and his scoring could now begin. It seemed a requirement that one keep drinking. After a turn, each player would resort to his glass for reward or consolation. Lolly's escort was drinking what looked like a suspiciously light beer and seemed content with sips, while the others refreshed themselves heartily with protracted chugs and generous gulps. The team with the advantage bought for those less lucky. Aaron felt slightly ashamed not only to be the cause of his team's poor standing but to accept one round after another from the hands of his more skilled opponents. The pig man, however, told him not to mind. He was a guest of the nation, of county Kerry. It would be a harsh blow to Irish hospitality if Aaron were to refuse.

The opponents won the first game easily. Aaron allowed himself to look over toward Lolly. She was observing her fingernails. The second game began. This time the score was kept a bit more even, with Aaron and the pig man getting the advantage from time to time. On a treble 20 and a double 3 by the pig man, they took the game. The third and final round began.

Lolly's escort and the suspendered fellow got the advantage quickly. Aaron felt disgrace lumbering toward him, a disgrace that would also sully the pig man, who deserved better. Lolly's friend hit a double 17, which, for reasons not completely clear to Aaron, was considered something of a triumph. Since applause was impossible for people holding a glass, the approval was expressed by expletive: "Aaah," "ooh," "good man," "fair play," and, inevitably, "The fucker did it." Aaron thought he heard an aah that sounded very much like the few aahs he'd heard from Lolly earlier in the day. He took yet another swig. He wanted Lolly to transfer her regard from her friend to himself. To make the decision official, he took a long and goodly gulp.

His next dart kissed the wire and bounced out. Then he scored a passable double 9. His third dart, for reasons not completely clear, hit a triple 19. He was given a few noises, more in surprise than in approval. He pulled his darts from the board and headed back behind the line. Lolly, he felt, was looking at him. He nodded. She made no move. She hadn't been looking at him but at the man she'd come in with. Aaron became possessed. With the pig man at his side, suggesting which numbers would best serve them, he let fly the darts, *unfailingly* scoring the needed points in the best possible order. The competition heated up. Murmurs were heard, but no aahs from Lolly. He would not look at her until the advantage was his and the pig man's. Then he would glance at her, not while retrieving his darts but immediately after the crucial points were made. With the accelerating pace expected of a truly good game, the score drew even, and then, as seemed destined, with Aaron's treble 19, he and the pig man gained the advantage.

Aaron glanced over his shoulder. Lolly was watching her friend, who was staring down in disbelief at the darts in his hand. He brushed the polys against his cheek, used them to scratch the tip of his well-shaped nose, then lowered his hand. He did not look back at Lolly. Lolly, however, continued to look at him. Warmth and sympathy were emanating not just from her gaze but from her whole body. Her posture, unthinking of itself, relaxed but clearly directed toward her friend, spoke a sad encouragement, a reassurance that defeat would not go unrewarded.

Meanwhile the pig man would tell him where to direct his aim, and he would follow the instruction. More pints were ordered, more pints were drunk. The end of the game approached.

By this time, because the underdogs were coming from so far behind and with a fatalistic advance usually reserved for a Beethoven symphony, the group of spectators had grown to a small crowd. Enough of the throng had left their pints behind so that applause was possible during these final moments. "His name's McCloud," was heard whispered more than once. "Aaron, they say," was heard as well as "Aaron McCloud, the nephew." He was also identified as "the one with the pig."

It was Aaron's turn. With 110 points remaining—with the required zero now mathematically possible, the pig man gave his instructions: a single 20, a triple 18, a double 18. Aaron took a moment simply to stare at the board. Surfacing from some clouded region deep in his brain was a different strategy that would be all his own: a treble 20, leaving 50 left. He would go out with a double bull.

No sounds were heard. Aaron toed the line, aimed and made the toss. The treble 20. A few gasps, then silence. A double bull and the world was his. Aaron took a deep breath. No one else seemed to breathe at all. He took aim, holding off until the board came completely into focus. Now he could see it clearly as if some final correction had been made not in his sight but in the board itself. He made the toss. Through the direct intervention of a power as yet unrevealed, the double bull was given.

Shouts, exclamations, oaths. Aaron was rushed to the bar, swept along by his admirers. His back was slapped and his buttocks too; his arms were squeezed, his hands clasped, his hair tousled, his cheeks patted—all the abuse that was his due was duly given. When he turned toward the room and raised his pint in salute to his newly won enthusiasts, he saw Lolly heading toward the door, alone. He noticed next that her friend was among those thronged around him, cheerful, celebrating his own defeat with sure delight and an upraised glass. Aaron tried to push through the crowd, but his effort was interpreted as an attempt to mingle humbly with his admirers. The back slaps and arm squeezes were repeated with increased aggression, and the girl in the pink T-shirt pulled his ear. Lolly was out the door. Aaron made one more push against the crowd, but to even less avail. This time a pint was thrust against his chest, the spilled stout pouring against his shirt, the cloth sticking to his skin. Now he smelled like sour coffee. The merriment that greeted the accident inspired the man in the yellow suspenders to pour an entire glass over Aaron's head. Another glass followed, then a third, all amid cheers and shouts of joy.

Through the falling stout that near-blinded his eyes, Aaron looked for the pig man to rescue him, but he was nowhere to be found, not in the crowd, not at the bar, not in the room.

Off to his right, Lolly's escort in the dark suit was staring down into his pint, a sly half smile on his face. Aaron saw as well the thin tie, dark, knotted loosely beneath the Adam's apple. He couldn't avoid noting the long strong fingers, nor could he ignore the heavy unshined shoes. Aaron looked at the face, the well-formed nose, straight but nicely rounded at the tip, the ample lips even more tumescent than his own, the cheeks taut over the high bones, the forehead made low by locks of hair loosened from the original slick. In his confused and drunken state, Aaron told himself the man was Declan Tovey. Acquainted as Aaron was with the skeleton, he had no difficulty putting flesh to the familiar bones. The suit, all the more dignified for being casually worn, was no longer hanging lank on the skeletal frame. The head held a full crop of hair and the shoes firmly touched the floor, weighted there by the reconstituted corpse, the blood hotly coursing, the arms and legs no longer scrawny but muscled hard underneath the solid, potent flesh.

Now Aaron knew why the man was smiling. He was smiling because he had effected this return. He was smiling because he knew that his destiny and the destiny of Lolly McKeever had been joined for all time to come. No relationship could be more intimate than theirs: the murdered to the murderer. No passion could equal the heated moments that had climaxed their alliance; no love could match the intensity of their final exchange. This softly smiling man, this Declan Tovey, would, by the deed done, by the murder, possess Lolly forever. No one could take his place; no one could aspire to his eminence. No one could wipe the sly smile from his face.

Aaron set his glass on the bar, shoved aside the girl in the T-shirt, lurched at the smiling man, and punched him in the nose. A second blow, intended to achieve a knockout, missed its mark when the man ducked. Aaron had smacked the man wearing the suspenders. Others intervened. A melee followed. Aaron had provided yet another pretext for being mauled, and those assembled took full advantage of the gift. The exchange of blows, however, was hardly limited to Aaron's person alone. The suspendered man was being kicked by the T-shirted girl, a gaunt man with close-cropped hair was pummeling a participant in a green sweater who, in turn, was swinging his arms wildly, hitting a matronly woman who banged her glass against the side of the gaunt man's head.

Francis—now out from behind the bar—was flailing his way to the center of the trouble. Aaron had pulled back to the bar, the better to observe. Declan, if indeed it was he, had moved closer to a booth and was, like Aaron, giving the brawl his disinterested attention. Aaron's eyes and the eyes of Declan met. They nodded courteously to each other, raised their respective glasses in mutual salute, and drank generously to each other's continuing good health.

The girl in the T-shirt was taken into the arms of the gaunt man, the suspendered man was sent back to a booth, the man in the green sweater was directed toward the Men's and the rest urged by Francis to step up to the bar for a pint on the house. Everyone did as he or she had been told. Aaron turned again to face Declan. The man was not where he'd been. Nor was he in one of the booths, nor at one of the tables or among those at the bar. Declan Tovey was gone.

Aaron considered making inquiries under the pretense that he wanted to apologize for the unprovoked attack. He would search the man out; there would be another meeting, words exchanged, the obvious made obvious: The man would prove not to be Declan. For the simple reason that he couldn't possibly be Declan. That Aaron had been destabilized by downing uncounted pints was not an acceptable explanation of the confusions.

A second thought that followed hard upon the first was that he must not make inquiries. He should not search out the man; he should not require enlightenments. Some things were better left unknown. Ignorance, however uneasy, was often a preferred condition. Through whatever power that holds sway over such matters, the man had gone. And this, Aaron suspected, was not a power over which he had much influence. Fairly certain was he that, like most forces lately introduced into his life, this one was inscrutable, beyond logic, given to the coincidental, fulfilling purposes of its own, satisfying needs known perhaps not even to itself, and totally indifferent to requests for explanation, knowledge, or understanding. As Great-Aunt Molly had said, "We move from one mystery to the next, and from this comes wisdom." For the first time in his life, he was beginning to believe that the good woman was right, and he must be Irish enough to accept it.

Aaron would have one more drink and head home. It was late. He was soaked and smelly—and not for the first time that day. The walk home would do him good. He would see the stars and feel the winds come down from the hills, the breezes wafting in from the sea. There would, of course, be scents and sights. There would, of course, be a moon. He would lift his soul to the sky and be transformed. It had not been an easy day, but it was over now, and he could surrender himself to the cosmic embrace the drink had prepared for him.

He raised his glass. He would empty it, then order the last

Guinness of the day. With the pint at his lips, the stout slurping into his mouth—with a little to spare for the front of his shirt—he saw, over the rim of his glass, the door to the bar inch open. It would be Declan, returned. It would be Lolly, come to make amends for her show of indifference. It could even be his aunt, summoned back from London to see him safely home. The door opened wider. Aaron took the pint from his lips. The pig entered, its snout high in the air as if sniffing out the presence it had come to seek.

It was as though the porcine man had gone to the nearest phone booth, shed his outer garment, and returned in his true form. The pig had been there all evening; it had instructed him in the game of darts and guided him to victory. It had decreed the postponement of his sorrows. It had shown him a good time and won him many worshippers. It had returned now to take him home.

Without hesitation the pig clattered across the wooden floor, its hooves tapping like the high heels of a pair of party girls stepping out for a dance. It stopped in the middle of the room and brushed its snout along a crack in the planks. Before any other thought could enter Aaron's mind, he became worried about splinters. He should call to the pig. But he knew it would be useless. The pig was nameless and not known for its acquiescence. Aaron knew what he must do. There was no alternative, no other possibility. He put his glass on the bar and, without looking either to his left or to his right, without paying tribute to the camaraderie he'd been awarded, he headed straight for the still-open door. From behind he heard the approaching clatter of cloven hoofs. He stepped outside and started down the road. The clatter continued, the *tippity-tap-tap*, an accompaniment that imposed a steadying rhythm on his walk.

He did not turn around. There was no need. Nothing now

could induce abandonment; nothing could create the sought-for solitude. The stars were of no use; the moon a simple convenience to light his way, the winds with their melodic waftings unable to compete with the determined metronomic clopping of the high heels pursuing yet guiding him, pressing him forward, despite his lurchings, toward a fate yet to be revealed, irresistible and beyond all refusal.

Resigned, Aaron raised his head, his heart, his voice in song, the melody borrowed from "For He's a Jolly Good Fellow":

> We let the pigs in the parlor,
> We let the pigs in the parlor,
> We let the pigs in the parloooorr —
> *And they are Irish, too!*

Stumble as he might, fall as he did, Aaron made a fairly straight path toward what awaited him, the *tippity-tap-tap*, the *clack* and the *clop* following faithfully after.

6

The following morning Aaron considered taking to the hills, to the low mountains rising to the east just above the town, where the moon's pull would not impose tidal restrictions on his time and force an ending, all too soon, to the day's sufferings. From the summit he could view the great world spread out before him, the parceled pastures sloping down to the fields that reached the headlands.

But there was a drawback. The hills had distractions of their own. It was his great-aunt Molly, who'd taken him time and time again to the summit, where they would move among the sheep, regarding the wool's growth, its texture, and its promise of plenty. The hills belonged to Aunt Molly. Not even Phila would be a match for her persisting presence. Just the idea that morning—before even getting out of bed, before thoughts of Phila, before confusions about Declan Tovey—just the thought of climbing the pastures up past the heather, through the furze and the rocks and the muddied paths to the waiting heights, had given him again the sight of his great-aunt, tall, indomitable, astride the summit, gesturing with an arm grand enough in its sweep to include all the lands below and speak to him the words that had struck into his soul and made him Irish forever, no matter what other allegiances he might claim.

"It was surely at this height," Aunt Molly had said, "it was at this height and at this place that the devil brought the proud powers of England and, speaking, said to them: 'All this will I give you' "—and here the gesture came—"'all this will I give you if you will but bow down and worship me.' And no sooner had the devil spoken these words than their knees, their English knees, buckled under them—and who would blame the poor hoors, such a height and such a wonder as was laid out before them? And so we fight not only to free ourselves but to free them too, don't forget. To get them up off their knees at last so they can stand and walk upright in the lovely land, free of the tempter's thrall. It's for them, for the kneeling English too, that we fight, poor hoors. And so it goes and goes and goes until we've freed them for good." But then she would laugh a great laugh and add: "Or for evil. For with them, you never know." Then she would sigh a heavy sigh and repeat, by way of an amen, "Poor hoors."

Not all that eager to renew his Irish credentials—not from infidelity or indifference but from a need to indulge emotions not quite so grand—Aaron chose the sea. Some other time he would give Aunt Molly her due.

Aunt Kitty had returned in the night. She was there, in the kitchen, working away at her computer while he fixed himself a full breakfast: two more hot dogs, a banana, and three cups of coffee that, in their black simplicity, were the perfect antidote for the sour Guinness of the night before. He felt, as it happened, quite fit. Kitty, for her part, concentrated on her writing, the man in the priest's room ignored completely. Each morning his aunt worked and nothing—nor life nor death—could persuade her away from her gleeful remediations. She had, for the moment, at the suggestion of her London publisher, abandoned Trollope's *Can You For-*

give Her? (she couldn't) and was concentrating on her correction of *Tess of the d'Urbervilles*, where the Tess character, now named Tiffany, kills not her first seducer—here named Kyle—who had provided for her and for her family but the husband who had rejected her when she revealed her past sins. This, Kitty had pointed out, was the rightful ending. *He*, the husband, was the one to be killed. She even kept the name of Clair, so it was Clair who would get run through with the sword, not someone of a substitute name. Ever since reading the book as a sixteen-year-old, Kitty had wanted Clair to get his just deserts, and she took particular pleasure in being on such intimate terms with the event that when it finally came about she was, as writer, not only present, but saw to it that the craven Clair was given his moment of unredeeming amazement when, with a conveniently provided sword, Tess/Tiffany nailed him to the headboard.

"Today's the day," Kitty had said as Aaron was eating his second hot dog. She rubbed her hands together to work up the heat appropriate for the deed she was about to do. "By the time you get back, he'll have had it, and bad cess to him." She quivered in anticipation, causing her shoulders to hunch and her elbows to draw themselves closer to her ribs. By the time the screen door slammed behind him, Aaron could hear the muted click of the computer keys hurrying Tiffany toward the revenge not only on the husband but on Thomas Hardy and a fair portion of nineteenth-century English literature as well. "Bad cess" was one of his aunt's favorite phrases.

To protect his feet from the stones and shells that paved the beach, Aaron had worn his sandals, but with a pair of white socks, because he felt self-conscious about the way his big toe was trying to crawl on top of the toe next to it. That he would meet anyone on the beach seemed unlikely; that he would meet anyone interested in his toes was even less likely; but, with the exception of matters of the heart, Aaron preferred not to take chances.

In the distance the waves boomed and cracked. Aaron advanced at what he considered a pace suitable to thought and to vacant-eyed meditation. Small stones poked sharply at the soles of his sandals, and occasionally a larger rock sent him lurching to the side, but he held to a mourner's slow stride.

About a hundred yards from the rock face of the intruding cliff, he saw a figure round the point, a man of some size, moving toward him with a determined step. As if performing an exercise intended to strengthen the calves, firm the buttocks, and give free swing to the arms, back and forth, the man seemed to be marching in response to an invisible military band. Now the arms were raised above his head as he scissored them back and forth across each other. Whether to attract Aaron's attention or to ward him off seemed only two of several possibilities. This could be part of the exercise. Or the man might be pursued by real or imagined furies invisible at the distance. He seemed to have picked up his pace, big arms waving more frantically until one arm flopped across his forehead and sent a hand dangling over his face. It was, of course, Kieran Sweeney.

Now his hands were cupped to each side of his mouth, and he seemed to be shouting something that Aaron's sea-deafened ears couldn't catch. Aaron, too, moved more quickly. Sweeney, giving up his attempt to communicate, stopped and stayed where he was. It would be up to Aaron to approach. He, Sweeney, had done all he'd intended to do and would do no more.

Aaron came up to him, limping slightly, "Didn't you see me waving?" Sweeney asked.

"Waving?" Aaron leaned his head closer. Sweeney was breathing hard and seemed somewhat impatient, his eyes wide, his teeth quite possibly clenched.

"Yes. Waving. I was waving."

"Yes. I saw you. Waving." Aaron nodded.

"And I was shouting."

"Yes. Shouting. I could tell you were shouting."

"And you kept right on anyway."

"Yes. Right on."

"But I was telling you to turn around. To go back."

"Oh. Go back. I was wondering what it was." Aaron nodded again.

"Then why didn't you? Turn back?"

"I'd come down for a walk."

"But can't you see the sea?"

"Yes. I can see it."

"Can't you see what it's doing?" he asked.

"See the water rising? The waves?"

"Those aren't waves. Look again. They're jaws or maws or whatever you like. See how they open wide, and then wider still? They're the mouths of monsters and they're after you."

"Me?"

"You."

"The waves may be high, yes, but they don't seem to come to shore."

"Of course they don't. They're taunting us. They're telling us what they have planned and what they're going to do."

"Oh?"

"And it won't be just a drowning. Look at the white along the crests. That's not froth. Those are teeth. Look now how the jaws clamp down. You're not drowned. You're devoured."

"Oh. I see."

"And you don't remember? It's you they've marked. Didn't I tell you? They made you their own yesterday. They're not just teasing. They'll be coming for you any minute now."

"When the tide comes in? But that's not for another hour."

"Do they look like they wait for tides? We could be standing right here where we are and before we could get from here to there we'd be swallowed whole."

"Then you're saying I should go back?"

"Do you want me to say it again?"

"Well. All right. But I did want to go for a walk."

"Then you must do it. And I'll say my farewells to you now since there'll be no other chance."

"Well. Good-bye, then." Aaron held out his hand.

Sweeney shook his head. "You're worse than your aunt. The curse of your race. They do what they want no matter. Well, it's an honorable way you've chosen to go. Good men have gone this way before. I can't say you're worthy of their company, but that's for the sea to decide."

"I'll turn back when the tide begins to come in, don't worry."

"No, I won't worry. It's all past worry. And you're not worse than your aunt. No one is worse than your aunt."

"Oh?"

"It's said in sorrow, not accusation. An observation, certifiable by all who know her. And it's said in anger and with more provocation than a man is meant to bear."

Sweeney had turned away, sending his gaze out over the sea. The booming thunders seemed to make him solitary. He spoke, the words hurled into the gaping maws. "It's a terrible thing to murder a man," he said. "Or so I suppose. A haunting thing to have done what can't be undone. The man's dead and she's done it and she'll never get free. And now she has him there in the house with her. It'd make a lesser woman mad, but not your aunt. Not she."

Aaron looked down at his socks and wiggled his toes. A great wave, closer to shore, slammed down into the tortured waters. He looked up at Sweeney. Sweeney, still staring out over the sea, as if searching for some sail he knew would never appear, lifted his head higher. A look of solemn mourning came into his face.

Aaron concentrated again on his feet. "My aunt says Lolly McKeever did it, Lolly says you did it, and you say—my aunt. You know what I think?"

"You think I did it." Aaron made no move. Sweeney continued. "Think that, if you like. It makes no matter." He turned, looked at Aaron, reached out, and took him by the arm. "Come," he said. "I can't let you stand here so close to your eternity. I'll walk you back."

"Thanks, but I'm going the other way."

"No. I can't let you do it."

"But it's what I came to do. To walk. Here. Along the beach. Alone."

"Yes," Sweeney said. "We walk the beach and look at the stones and let the sea think we don't know it's there. We walk and let the sorrows come. We let the sea do all the raging for us so we can be gentle to ourselves in our suffering. We let the sea do our yearning." He lowered his head. "All right, then. Go on. It's a great grave you'll have and the company, if not of saints then at least the nibbled dead, to welcome you. The mouth of the fish is better than the mouth of the worm and not so noisy, I'm told."

He went past Aaron but stopped after two steps. Without turning around, he said, "Is it a wife you've lost or what?"

"A woman."

"Beautiful?"

"Not particularly."

"And you thought she'd be grateful to get a man so splendid."

"Yes."

"But she wasn't grateful."

"No."

Sweeney nodded. "Ingrates, all of them. No idea of the bounty being offered."

"You're here for the same reason?"

"Ingrates. Maybe not all of them. But one of them I will never name."

"Is it a name I know?"

"No man knows the names I have for her."

"But does she know, this woman, does she know the way you feel?"

"No one knows how I feel."

"Does she have any idea?"

"Idea? How could she? It's beyond all imagining."

"Maybe you could give her some hint."

"And what good would that do?"

"She might think it rather a fine thing."

"No, not she. Never."

"But why?"

"Because it's not a fine thing. It's a madness."

"But why?"

"She's my enemy from birth. And I am hers. We were brought into this world to take on the enmity left behind from years long gone. Our baptismal vows are nothing compared to the oath we take with the first light we see and the first cry we make. An oath not in water but in blood. Forgotten blood of long ago. All that survives is the enmity. And don't say it isn't there. It is. I have it. She has it. We exchange it back and forth. We can't let it go, because that would be surrendering who we are. We'd be no one without it. It's what gives us life. And we wouldn't trade it for all the love the world has to give. This world and the next."

"But can't you———"

"No. I can't. And she can't."

"Then that settles it, doesn't it?"

"It's settled. Yes."

Aaron's feet were getting cold. He looked down to see why this should be and saw the water receding from the beach, flowing over his toes, wetting his socks. He stared a moment, then looked straight ahead. The rock face, the wall cleaving the sea, still rose up in the distance, shadowed by a passing cloud. The clouds hadn't moved before but were moving now, not swiftly but with a confidence suggesting that a command had been given and they were on the march. Another wave came in, small, gentle, no more than a light laugh. It ran up and surrounded Aaron's ankles, then, delighted with its mischief, retreated back into the sea.

"If I'm going to continue my walk, I'd better start," Aaron said.

He took a few steps and stopped. Sweeney was saying something, but the waves had increased their fury and seemed to be making a more determined advance to the shore, and Aaron could barely hear. He considered going back within hearing distance but knew if he was going to have any time with Phila, it would have to be now. He didn't think it admissible to postpone it another day. The poor woman had been neglected enough as it was. He'd had almost no thought of her since he'd come to Kerry, and this was hardly fair. Kerry was meant to feed his grief, to bring his self-pity to the highest possible pitch and allow him to send his wailings upward, at one with the shrieks of the gulls and the curlew's cry. But all his fine intentions kept being thwarted. If he were so inclined and if he could convince himself no one could see, he'd stamp his foot, wet sock and all. Instead he resolved to resume his walk, and Sweeney could stay there blathering on about love and death to his heart's distress. Aaron, for his part, had his own suffering to consider, and he would be faithful.

Down the beach he went, determined not to notice the rising billows. He thought he heard Sweeney behind him, shouting, "Her name is——" And the last word was lost to the sound of the sea, where, about fifty feet from shore, was the sight of what looked like a canoe with a man paddling almost lazily, as if making his way down a smooth flowing river. Now he was rising, taken to the top of an angry swell, now he disappeared only to be raised high again, in full view, as the waves lifted and dropped him.

Then the canoe was on the crest of a wave, and as the paddler leaned down toward the water, his arm shot out, reaching for something. The canoe and the man were dropped down behind the advancing wave. Aaron saw, held high on the crest just before it crashed, the man's paddle.

The canoe reappeared, the man sitting calmly upright, looking neither to the shore nor to the advancing sea. He seemed to have placed his hands, folded, in front of him on his knees. He could be praying or simply waiting, patiently, for what was soon to happen. Aaron recognized him. He was none other, of course, than his opponent of the night before, the imagined Declan Tovey, the suitor, real or imagined, of Lolly McKeever, the man whose nose Aaron had punched.

Twice the man appeared, and twice disappeared. All movement was the sea's, he himself moved not at all. Aaron turned his face to the north and took five paces. The wind had filled his shirt; now it swelled behind him like a great white hump, a disfiguring burden instead of a blown sail. He took another five steps, then another three. The canoe was tilted to a forty-five-degree angle, no longer riding from crest to trough to crest again, but caught at last in the rising maw, the froth-toothed mouth ready to close down and swallow its prey. Down the crashing water came, sending its wild spume toward shore. The canoe reappeared, the man still inside. Just as he had refolded his hands, another mouth closed down.

Aaron ripped open the cuffs and front of his shirt, sending garment and buttons flying in a single backward fling. He rid himself of his khaki shorts. Now clad only in his cotton briefs, he rushed into the water and dived into the first wave that came for him. Immediately he dropped down to a depth where his feet failed to touch bottom. To resist the cold more than to survive the water, he stroked out ahead with his arms and, with legs and feet, performed an unending series of entrechats that would have been the envy of the greatest *danseur noble* now performing on the planet. Propelled by the unceasing beat of his feet, pulled forward by the unthinking stroke and lunge of his arms, he made his way through wave after wave, rising, falling, straining forward, insistent that he do nothing but advance until he reached the doomed canoe.

Walls of water rose ahead, great swellings passed under him; twice he was tumbled and twice he recovered. The salt taste in his mouth told him he'd taken on water. Still he continued what he hoped was forward, closer, closer to the man he was determined to save.

At the rise of a medium swell he saw about fifteen feet to his left, the canoe, now nosed toward the shore, the man not looking in his direction or even taking note of the change in the canoe's course. His hands were no longer folded, but gliding through the water at the canoe's sides. Before Aaron could call out, another wave tumbled down on top of him and it seemed, as he struggled to reach the air above, that the sea had finally made its claim and he should cease and desist in his futile defiance.

He swallowed water and struggled harder, his arms heavy from the weight of his hands, his legs weary from the drag of his feet. He must throw off this heaviness. He must fling from him his hands and shake his ankles free of his feet. Flinging, shaking, he reached the air. He pulled it in, but it gagged him. And another wave tumbled down, dunking his head, holding it under, not even offering to free him after the count of ten. Again he took up his struggles, cursing the hugeness of his weighted hands, begging to be free of his size twelve feet. Again his mouth was flooded with the salty taste stinging the inside of his nose, threatening to burst open his ears so the water could make a more thorough invasion. But the air was near, then nearer. His hands became as light as down; his feet buoyant, lifting him toward the blessed air he was to be given at last.

First he felt the water rush from his mouth. There was a taste of sand on his tongue, a sea taste of weed and kelp. Next he felt the waves press down on his chest and water spurt out of his mouth. Again a wave pressed down. He twitched his hands. He shifted his feet. There was no water under him. This then, was the ocean's bed, and he had come to rest on it and wait for the murmuring currents and the whispering nibbles that would relieve him of his flesh and heart and lungs, his liver and his spleen, that would unman his proud and lovely crotch, that would transform him to Declan Tovey's twin, bare bones clothed not even in tatters, scalped, without even a Brewers baseball cap to cover his head. Unmourned he would lie, and unmournful too. Phila would cease to matter. Lost. All lost. Due to the imagined look-alike of the dead Declan Tovey, out in his canoe.

Again a great wave pressed down on him, but this time it forced him to take in what seemed to be air, not water. The wave pressed down again and again. He felt his opened mouth sucking in some drying substance not unlike the breath he had known and been accustomed to during his life on earth. He opened his eyes. A wet tangle of weeds, brownish yellow turning to green, was less than six inches from his nose. It had the smell of fish no longer fresh. The leaves looked like the emptied seed pods from a maple tree, interspersed at intervals with what seemed oblong beads growing a slimy fur, a sea rosary sent to tempt him to prayer.

The pressure was repeated. Aaron grunted. In quick succession three more shoves were made downward on his sides, along his ribs. "Hah! Now you've done it!" a voice said. "You've gone and saved him." It was a man's voice, a voice that managed to be both amused and unbelieving at the same time. "And are you all right? You took on a bit of water yourself, you know."

"I'll be all right by the end of the day," another voice said, this one low and solemn, the breath coming in quick gasps between the words. Aaron lifted his head with the intention of twisting it around so he could see who was there and ask what was happening and what had happened that had brought him here, lying on the sand with a tangle of kelp inches from his nose. That he had failed to save the man in the canoe and that he himself had been rescued was apparent to him now, but a few particulars might be welcome. He felt a hand on his shoulder encouraging him to put his head back down on the sand. "Rest yourself another minute," the quiet, solemn voice said.

Aaron obediently put his head back down and stared at the seaweed. A sea spider was coming toward him, making its way from bead to bead, walking more along the side than the top, the long, hair-thin legs barely touching the furred surface as it moved. Aaron had never realized how tiny the body itself was and how extended and delicate were the legs that took the body to wherever it might want to go. When the spider was less than three inches from Aaron's nose, he lifted his head again and, before he could be urged to do otherwise, he raised his right shoulder and turned to look at his rescuer.

There, seated on the rock, was Sweeney, naked, his elbows propped on his knees, his head bowed into his hands, his torso heaving slowly up and down as if he were keening, but without a wail or a moan. Water dripped from his hair onto his hands and ran in rivulets between the knuckles and down past his wrists to his knees where they disappeared in the thick red hair that sprang from his shins and calves.

Aaron, still stiff in the arms and legs and spine, got up and stood watching, wondering what he might say or do. Then he saw the man he'd attempted to rescue standing ten feet off, the paddle of the canoe held like a staff in his right hand, the canoe nosing his leg like a faithful pet. He was looking at Aaron. His lips were jutted forward. His eyes were wide and round and seemed amused by what they saw. Aaron thought the time had come to punch his nose again. He lurched toward the man but stumbled when the numbness in his legs absorbed without effect the signals sent out by the will.

"This is not one of the better places to take a swim," the man said. "There are plenty of better beaches, in case you have any trouble like the trouble you've had today. You're a lucky man. And did you know you're still wearing socks?"

To rob the man of any further satisfaction, Aaron turned away and went toward Sweeney. Sweeney had lowered his hands from his face and was letting them dangle between his knees, not quite shielding the plump penis and low-hanging testicles that sloped along the curve of the stone where he sat. The heaving breaths had become less labored. He was staring out over the water, his mouth slightly open, his eyes quiet and mournful. His exhaustion had brought him to a repose where neither rage nor exasperations could hide his sorrow.

Aaron went no closer. He started to turn, back toward the man with the pet canoe, but decided to do as Sweeney was doing, to stare out over the sea.

Finally Sweeney spoke. "I should never have done it," he said. "I'll never be forgiven. Never at all."

Aaron said nothing. Sweeney was talking to the sea, not to him. It would be impolite to insinuate himself into the conversation. He'd wait until Sweeney addressed him directly. And there, behold, he saw, well offshore, the canoe, the man paddling his way out into the rising, the falling waves.

"He's doing it again!" Aaron must have meant to shout, but it all came out more like a moan. To test his ability to modulate, he repeated "He's doing it again!" The modulation was there, effected mostly by a gagging in his throat, then a gargling, then a thin line of water emerging from his mouth and running down his chin onto his chest. "Look! There!" he said in a hoarse whisper. "Look!"

"I've betrayed my name," Sweeney said in reply. "I've dishonored my family for all time to come. And may I never be forgiven."

Aaron turned to face the mournful man. He was standing, still naked except for the thick reddish hair that covered his chest and the thick orange hair that curled around the base of his dick and the darker hair that furred the skin of his balls. Without acknowledging Aaron's presence, he continued to stare out toward the rampage before him. Aaron was tempted to ask what he might be talking about, but before be could say anything, Sweeney spoke again. "My name is Kieran Sweeney and your name is Aaron Mc-Cloud. And you were meant to drown, and I was meant to watch and see it happen. But I didn't watch. I saw the waves claiming you for their own, and rightly so. I've told you that. But, no, being a McCloud, you hear nothing a Sweeney says. In you go—and the waves waiting, moving their jaws up and down. This was as it was meant to be. And it was meant to be that I would see it and rejoice. But did I rejoice or even smile? No. I, Kieran Sweeney, unstable of mind and with a body beyond all control, went running in, fighting the waves like the heroes we Sweeneys always were and are and will always be. And I reach down and drag you up from where they've caught you, from where you belong. And not content to simply laugh in your face and let you go, I pull you out of the depths. And then do I just fling you down and let you die? No. Unstable of mind, I work away and send the water gushing out of you onto the stones. And you're a McCloud. McCloud, do you hear? A cursed McCloud. And I a good and blessed Sweeney. An enemy in the blood, an enemy in the breath. From all time past and all time to come. And I saved you, so I'm cursed along with you and with you all!"

Aaron did little during the tirade except blink and let his lower lip fall a bit lower, little by little. But now the lip could go no lower, the jaw could fall no farther. His amazement was complete. He blinked once more, with Sweeney still standing huge before him, the cliffs and the scree rising high behind him, blackened red and darkening rust. It was his aunt whom Sweeney loved, that he already knew. And for Kitty McCloud did Sweeney walk the shore grieving and sorrowing. She was one of the cursed, born on the far side of a boundary that must never be crossed, and he a man too foolish to kick the nonsense aside and say what was in his heart. Aaron decided to speak.

"Does my aunt know that you're in love with her?"

Sweeney curled the fingers of his right hand into a fist, but made no other move. Slowly he let the fingers uncurl. After they had rested a moment, lightly touching his thighs, he said—without looking at Aaron—"See him out there, getting farther and farther from shore. The paddle will be taken from him again. The water will come into the boat. Lower it will go until there's no hope for it. And the man will go under. But you—you must go for him. Save him. Do again what you already did. Try to rescue him. Please. Try again. And this time I will watch and keep on watching. Maybe he'll keep his canoe again and make it to the shore. But you, you must go under and stay where you belong. No one must come for you. No one must save you. Please. I promise by my family's good and blessed name I'll make no move. My mind I'll feed with ancient thoughts, my body I'll instruct to stand where it stands. You'll drown—you'll drown! And I watching! And I'll be the one saved. See? See there? His paddle's gone. He's adrift. Save him. Save him. And save me as well. You can do that, can't you?" Sweeney had moved closer, his, plea streaming from his eyes, near to taking the form of tears. "I saved you," he whispered. "Now you must save me."

"Why don't you just tell her you love her?"

Sweeney drew in a deep breath and sneered. "Of course you won't save me. You're a McCloud. A McCloud never saved anyone. I should have known better than to have asked."

"Maybe she feels the same way about you."

The sneer fell from his face, the jaw went slack, and the mouth opened. Then all was clamped shut again, with a look of loathing and disgust. Aaron waited for Sweeney to spit at him. But Sweeney merely turned and, with heavy tread, began to march more than walk, away to the north.

"Your clothes," Aaron called. "You forgot your clothes." Back Sweeney came. He reached down and gathered his pants and shirt and shoes and socks and undershorts and bundled them against his chest. Without looking at Aaron, he said, "Tell your aunt she had her chance to give proper burial to the dead. I'll be over before the day is done and take the man away. It's best she be rid of him. And tell her again her secret's safe with me. She did what she had to do, and not even Kieran Sweeney will blame her for it. But warn her I'm coming—and Declan Tovey goes with me." He turned north and began again his determined march. As Aaron watched, he saw a shoe drop from the bundle.

"Your shoe," Aaron called.

Sweeney stopped, stood a moment, then continued on.

"She loves you!" he yelled.

Sweeney went right on, the gulls careering overhead, the waves booming, and the waters hissing along the shore. Aaron considered picking up the shoe—to give it to him later—after all, he did save his life—but Sweeney might come back for it later when there was no one to see his need for it. Aaron turned and started south, toward home.

Then he realized that he himself was near to naked. He went back, retrieved his clothes and put them on, except the sandals. They were gone. The wind caught the loose shirt, the buttons flown, and flapped it out behind. Just before the shoreline made a curve at the foot of the cliffs, he took one more backward glance. Sweeney's shoe was still there, and Sweeney was nowhere in sight.

7

Kitty and Aaron and Lolly, like relatives around a sickbed, had gathered again in the priest's room to look down with solemn concern at the outstretched Declan Tovey. Declan, for his part, seemed neither the worse nor the better for having been left alone for almost twenty-four hours, except the grin seemed not quite so insolent, a bit more subdued than Aaron remembered. Like any patient surrounded by those discussing his fate, indifferent to his presence, involved solely in their own determinations, Declan seemed to have retreated into concerns considerably distant from the urgencies and intensities being exchanged not two feet from where he lay.

Lolly was already at the house when Aaron had returned from his dousing, wet again, cold again, but with the chattering and shivering under considerably more control than on the day before. Aaron had wanted to say something about the previous evening at Dockery's, starting not with a mention of his championship or even of the Declan surrogate accompanying her, but with a humble apology for his drunken state. Not that he cared one way or the other about his drinking, but it seemed a polite and possible pretext for beginning a review of an evening that had raised more than a few questions as yet unanswered. Who was the man? Why had Lolly not seen him, Aaron? Had she seen him but ignored him? Had she forgotten that they'd met that very afternoon in the presence of the present corpse? Perhaps she couldn't recognize him if he wasn't bedraggled, as he was now after his near drowning. All these he considered topics of high import, subjects that easily took precedence over what to do with the skeleton arrayed before them or the resolution of the unsolved matter of his murder. But Lolly, coming through the kitchen door had, at the sight of Aaron, merely said, "You've been swimming again. You'll catch your death." And had then swept past Kitty at her computer and into the priest's room, holding up a needle threaded with heavy black thread. Kitty and Aaron had followed. Lolly was already at work sewing the detached button back onto the man's coat, her hands supple and swift and obviously more competent at a domestic task than Aaron had considered likely.

"Tell Kieran Sweeney," she had said, "tell him the button is sewn back and he can give up being critical of the way things are being done."

It was at that point that Aaron—all his questions as yet unaddressed—had decided to tell in sequence the more than several amazements visited upon him within the past hour. But he couldn't quite reconstruct the exact order of things, his near-drowning after his own attempt to save Lolly's friend, or his determination that Sweeney was the murderer, convicted yesterday by the specifics given in his accusation of Kitty. Or was it Sweeney's hopeless love for Kitty? Or—and this he had already forgotten—Sweeney's rescue of him and the man's despairing regrets that he had saved a McCloud. Unable to untangle the events, he simply blurted out what he considered to be of greatest urgency. "Kieran Sweeney is in love with you."

Both women gasped. Lolly was again the first to find a word. "Me?" she cried.

"No," Aaron said. "You. Kitty."

"Me?!" She put her hand to her throat.

"You."

"Her?" asked Lolly, not disbelieving so much as surprised that she had not, by right, been given the preference.

"Her," said Aaron.

"The man is daft. And a Sweeney besides," said Kitty. "You're imagining things again."

"No. I'm not. I swear I'm not."

"And did he say the words himself?"

"It was clear enough without the actual words."

"I don't want to hear." Kitty shivered either to fight off the advances of a man so repellent or, more likely, to stifle the impulse to giggle. "He hates me as much as I hate him. If such is possible."

Aaron watched his aunt's face shed all feeling, the features assuming a noncommittal, bland aspect as if she were posing for a passport photo. She was inviting Aaron to observe her indifference. He dutifully observed, then looked down at the floor.

"He saved my life," Aaron said.

"He didn't save your life."

"He saved my life. I was drowning."

"How could you be drowning?"

"I was trying to save a friend of Lolly's."

Lolly had pulled the button, now sewn onto the jacket, up to her mouth and took the thread between her teeth. She was about to snap it, but not before she'd said, "What friend?"

"That man. The one you were with in Dockery's last night. Oily hair. A sort of runt, I thought."

"Who was in Dockery's?"

"You. With him. The runt."

"I? In Dockery's?"

"Last night. I was there. I played darts. I won."

"Well. Sorry I wasn't there for the event."

"But I saw you."

"Not me you saw. And I have no runt friends. Disgusting. Me? With a man like that? Me?"

"Well, actually, he was, I guess, for some maybe—well, maybe he was really not such a bad-looking guy. And—and just because he's shorter than I am——"

Lolly looked at Kitty, the thread not bitten through. "He's mad, your nephew. He's seeing things that were never there."

"Imagining things, too. Saved by a Sweeney. Have you ever heard the like?"

"But I *was* saved. And I did try to—I mean—the man from Dockery's. I won the dart game. Ask anybody. You were there, but you left. Then I beat him at darts, and he didn't drown anyway. Don't ask me how. He was in a canoe. But without a paddle. And Sweeney's in love with you. And—and . . ."

Aaron let his voice trail off, not because he'd finished his protest but because he'd been given a sudden truth: Lolly hadn't cut her hair. It was long, as long as it had been yesterday. Nor was it as severe as he remembered it being last night. He'd been mistaken. The dim light in Dockery's had allowed him—encouraged him—to see Lolly. But it hadn't been Lolly. And she hadn't been there with the man in the canoe, the man whose nose he'd punched. For whatever reason, he was relieved.

"Yes, yes, yes," his aunt was saying. "All right, all right, all right. Nobody's disagreeing. Are we, Lolly?"

"No. It's the truth itself if ever I heard it."

"All right, then," said Aaron, quite content to let the subject drop. "But I'll tell you something else. It was Sweeney did the murder."

Lolly was patting the button down, making sure it was in place on the dead man's jacket. She stopped. Kitty lowered her hand from her chest where it had gone after clutching her throat. She let it flop onto the bed near Declan's thighbone.

"He did it," said Aaron. "I know it. And I'm telling you now."

"And he—Sweeney—he said as much?" Lolly let her hand slip away from the button and rest on the skeleton's pelvis.

"No. But I could tell. The way he knew how it was done. The way it happened. He was, of course, accusing you while he was saying it."

"Me?" said Lolly.

"No. You. Kitty."

Kitty calmly straightened Declan's tie. "Of course he'd say a thing like that. Especially since he's so godawful in love with me."

"He even named the murder weapon. A tool in that bag. A—what's its name?"

"A leggett." Again Kitty and Lolly spoke at the same time.

"Yes. A leggett." Aaron paused, then asked, "How did you both know that?"

Kitty shrugged. Lolly extended her pursed lips, puckering them outward, then drew them in again. Neither woman said anything. Now Lolly straightened the tie and Kitty patted the button.

"Well," Aaron said. "Believe me or don't believe me. It'll all be over soon. Sweeney said he's coming to take away the—the—he's coming for Declan Tovey. To take him away. To bury him proper, he said."

"He won't!" said Lolly.

"He can't! said Kitty.

They both began smoothing out the blanket, proving themselves to be competent caregivers, concerned with the welfare of the patient. Lolly brought the blanket up to Declan's chest. Kitty folded it neatly back.

"He sounded determined," Aaron said.

"Hah!" Lolly managed to get more contempt into one syllable than Aaron had ever thought possible. Kitty's contribution was limited to a small smile and a sly look in the eyes, narrowing them and bringing the lids down almost halfway. "I can't wait," she said.

Nor did she have to. There was the sound of wheels on the gravel outside, then a growling halt.

"He's here," Aaron said.

"Oh, my God," said Lolly.

Kitty moved away from the bed. "He'll never so much as see him," she said.

"But," said Lolly, "he'll come in. Respect he has none of it. Not even for the priest's room." She looked down at Declan. She seemed about to throw herself on the corpse, a sacrificial effort to hide and protect it.

"But why," asked Aaron, "why can't you just let him take it— if you're not going to give it to the *gardaí*?"

Lolly put her hand to her throat, scandalized; Kitty shook her head wearily, her preferred gesture of contempt.

"It would save all of us all this trouble and——"

"In one breath," said Kitty, "you say he murdered the man. In the next you say hand him over, give him all the evidence against him. And where's the consistency in that?"

"Then at least let him see that we know what he's done; that we're the ones with the evidence. Let him come in. Let him see."

"Aaron," said Kitty sternly. "Don't interfere with things you know nothing about. We do not, on principle, let a Sweeney do as a Sweeney wishes." She had moved over to the crucifix on the spindly table. "Now," she said, "swear now, both of you, swear you never saw what you're going to see now."

Aaron stood up straighter. "Swear?"

"Swear. Both of you. Not out loud if you don't want to, but swear. You never saw what you're going to see."

With her fingernails she withdrew the nail from the left hand of the corpus on the cross. The hand stayed in place. She came back to the bed and reached up to where the oval picture had been hanging. Slowly she inserted the nail into the tiny hole where the original nail had been put into the wall. She took her fingers away and banged with her fist on the wall just to the left of the headboard. After listening a moment, she withdrew the nail and inserted it again. Again she listened. Again there seemed to be no response to what she'd done. After another moment she quickly pulled the nail out. "Of course. Wrong hand."

The slam of the truck door rattled the shuttered window. "Oh," said Lolly, her tone of voice close to a warning. Kitty had gone back to the crucifix, replaced the nail into the left hand, and withdrawn the nail from the right. This time the hand slipped slightly but stayed stuck to the wooden crossbeam. Kitty went to the wall, looked down at Declan Tovey as if to make sure he was all right, then put the nail into the wall. Immediately there was a click. Kitty banged again on the wall. Nothing. She banged again, lower down. A slow scraping sound was heard. Kitty moved back from the wall.

Aaron recognized the sound. It was the monster's scaly flesh rubbing against the tunnel walls, the beast coming closer and closer with each repeated scrape. The imagined sound of his childhood had become real, even to the steady increase of the noise as the monster continued its approach. As Aaron watched, a section of the wainscoting to the left of the bed—about three feet by three feet—slowly scraped open. A stench carried on a cold wind flooded the room. It was as if the sea itself had died and been left to rot. Putrid kelp and other seaweed sent their complaints into the room. Aaron felt that the room had sunk down to the depths of the decomposing sea and been left there untouched, unmoved, for years, taking into itself the depth and corruption of the long-buried waves, a chamber preserved for those chosen to know that even the sea would, at the last, molder and turn to rot. The wind stirred the bottom sheet near Declan Tovey's shoulder and pressed Aaron's salted clothes again against his flesh, sending their damp into his bones and, along the way, shivering his arms and forcing his legs to twitch.

This was the priests' tunnel to the beach. From here they had made their escape. The great secret of the house, denied him from his childhood on, had at last been revealed. Aaron resisted covering his nose. Long had he wanted to know what he now knew, long had he yearned to see what he now saw. To resist in any way whatsoever would be a sign of ingratitude, and he would not diminish his sense of wonder with the least display of distress. To prove himself worthy of the revelation, he purposely took in a deep breath, taking into his nose and into his lungs as much as he could of the putrefaction that assailed him now. He felt faint and reached out to steady himself on Declan Tovey's foot. The leather was gummy at his touch, the flesh of the foot perhaps still stuffed inside, but he kept his hold, so great was his need not to fall in a heap.

Lolly had covered her ears even though the assault had been to the nose. Next she clamped her hands over her mouth, then wrung the hands together in front of her breasts, and finally acknowledged the source of the attack by pinching shut her nostrils and saying, "Pee-yu."

Waving her hand back and forth in front of the tunnel opening, Kitty seemed more to be fanning a flame than forcing back into the dark the ghastly stink that by now had filled the room. Accepting her attempts as useless, she simply stopped, put her hand to her forehead to test for fever, then said, "We'll put him in here." She pulled a flashlight from the cabinet drawer, an old tin one. She held it out to Aaron. "Here."

Aaron took the flashlight. "You want me to get in there?"

"And move back, but careful, it goes downhill fast, and it smells like slippery. But hurry. Lolly and I will hand him in."

Aaron poked his head into the hole. The stink slammed into his face. Bent double, he stepped inside. Now the stink possessed him. He would become part of the rot. He beamed the flashlight ahead of him. It caught the slant leading down. He angled the light and saw, or thought he could see, a narrow stairway of rough-hewn stones that made a quick descent, then curved off to the left. As expected, the stones were slippery, but the crude cut, creating peaks and hollows, made a firm hold possible. He went down five steps, then turned, aiming the light back up toward the entry.

"Okay," he whispered. "Hand him in."

There was no echo, no reverberations. The dark growths on the steps and the walls absorbed all the sound as if the passageway were lined with felt. This helped him realize that he was being stifled. No air seemed to be coming in through the opening ahead of him, the gases surrounding him made impenetrable—almost solid—by the pollutants that seemed to be feeding on his flesh. "Hurry," he said, not bothering to whisper. "I can't breathe."

"Oh, shut up," his aunt said. "We're the ones doing all the work."

Aaron could hear a discreet rattling.

"Easy now," Lolly was saying. "We don't want to make him all a jumble, do we?"

"Keep the sheet stretched," his aunt said.

"Then don't come so close. Stay on your side."

"It's you bending the sheet."

"Pull back."

"Climb over the bed. Just step on the mattress. Go ahead."

The sound that followed was of a cascade of bones clattering together, falling against one another, some obviously dropping to the floor.

"Now you've done it."

"You didn't lift your side."

"Don't step there. Mind his arm."

"It's his leg."

"Mind his leg."

"Put it back in his pants, there, above the shoe."

Aaron tried to see what was happening, but the backside of his aunt had appropriated most of the opening. She was bent down and moving what seemed like her right arm. Swaying lightly, she kept working the arm.

"We can straighten him out when we get him inside." It was Lolly who spoke. Then she began to giggle. "So intimate, isn't it? Do you suppose he knows we're handling him all over the place?"

"Of course he knows. Or what's a heaven for?" His aunt managed to keep her severity.

Aaron coughed. "Can we hurry? I can't last much longer."

"Listen to him." Kitty said. "We're doing all the gruesome and he's the one complaining."

"I can't breathe."

"Then don't."

Kitty held the joined corners of the sheet in through the opening. With his free hand, Aaron took hold and backed onto the landing leading to the steps. The rest of the sheet followed, slung low with some sharp, some rounded thrustings poking against the linen.

"Quick. Back farther. There's more of him."

Aaron had to go two steps down. The body kept coming. Aaron could not remember the man being this tall.

"Okay. That's far enough. That's all there is." Lolly had taken over the opening and almost reverently set down her end. Aaron took one more step back and set down the corners he held. He intended to open the sheet, but the narrow passage allowed only room for the folded shroud.

Aaron raised his foot to start the climb back up the opening but could see no place to set it down. Declan Tovey took up all the room on the narrow stairs. He put his foot back on his own step and considered what to do, shove the bones to the side or just go ahead and step on them. The anticipated crunch gave him a quick shiver.

There was the sound of a heavy knock, loud enough to carry even into the recesses of the secret tunnel. "Quick," his aunt whispered. "We have to close the panel."

"I've come for my friend Declan. Hand him over." It was Sweeney's voice coming through the kitchen door. Aaron bent down to shove the shroud, but before he had touched the cloth, his aunt hissed the words, "Stay there. We'll be back." With that the panel was slammed shut. Aaron stared up the steps at the dark where the opening had been.

"No! Wait!" Aaron called, but there was no answer. He aimed the flashlight at the closed panel, searching along its surface for some handle or latch by which it could be opened. There was nothing. Slowly he moved the beam of light along the edges where the wood met the stone, then at the center, then again at the sides. The seal was absolute.

He knew now he was expected to stay where he was. His aunt was using him badly. He was being taken advantage of because of his good nature and his willingness to oblige. This was not acceptable. Sweeney or no Sweeney, he would crunch his way to the top of the steps and pound on the panel. He would not accept this entombment. He would not allow his beloved aunt so easily to maltreat him even in the service of a centuries-old family secret. If Sweeney wanted the bones, let him have them. The whole matter should be turned over to the police, to the *gardaí*, anyway.

As if to confirm the sad fact, Aaron reached down and folded back the sheet, to expose at least the skull, as if to give the poor man a chance to breathe. It was a headless corpse that confronted him, the collar of the tattered shirt completely uninhabited. Aaron parted more of the sheet. He found the cap just above the belt and the head just below. Aaron would not take the time to re-construct the man entirely, but the least he could do was put the man's head on right. When he lifted the skull, however, he sent a hand clattering down the steps. He froze where he stood. He lis-tened to hear if there was any response from the other side of the panel. He waited. He heard nothing. He had started to straighten up, the skull in his hand, when he heard Kieran Sweeney, distant but distinct, saying "I'm coming in to get him. I know he's there."

"No Sweeney sets a foot inside this house. You know that and I know that."

"I've come for my friend, and I won't be turned away. Poor man buried all this time in unholy ground. Shame. Shame."

It was Lolly's voice Aaron heard next. "Let him in, why not? He's raving, and there's no Declan Tovey here that he's referring to. Prove him wrong. When there's nothing to hide, why hide it?"

"He's a Sweeney," Kitty said.

"And never," said Sweeney, "would I dirty the soles of my shoes in such a place except to rescue my friend from his mur-derer."

"Then come in, Kieran Sweeney, and show me that anyone's been murdered. Come in. Don't keep hanging your fool of a face outside the door. It's open. Come in and welcome, and remind me to have Father Colavin come and bring the holy water when you've gone."

Aaron heard the slam of the screen door. "It hurts my feet to step inside, but I've done it." Sweeney spoke in a hoarse whisper. "And may I be forgiven."

"Just shut up, and don't go bumping into things and crashing everything down onto the floor."

"Can I be allowed to do my duty in silence?"

"Silence is the preferred speech when a Sweeney's doing the talking."

Heavy footsteps, booted, deliberate, seemed to come toward Aaron, then recede down the hall and up the stairs.

He put the skull on the step just below the collar, then retrieved the hand. When he slipped it partly into the sleeve, it angled away to the right, looking as if it was thumbing a ride. He straightened it out, but again it slid to the right, drawn downward by the descending steps. Convinced at first that the man himself, that Declan Tovey was doing all in his power to thwart his efforts made in the name of simple respect, Aaron considered letting the body lie in this ludicrous position, stretched out on the landing, with the upper torso two steps down, the head fallen to the third. He saw the detached skull as something of a plea, an appeal that he, Aaron, put the man right, that he separate and rearrange the bones until they formed the suggestion of a man with all his remaining parts, bare and disconnected though they might be, properly placed in relationship to one another, and restored to the dignity and reverence any skeleton surely deserved. As he set about the task, dexterously manipulating the flashlight and the bones, the flashlight and the clothing, he began to wonder why the provident plotter who had brought him to this dank and reeking place, dark and fetid, couldn't have arranged for Lolly Mc-Keever to have been shut up with him. Together they could have rearranged Declan Tovey. Together they could have found amusement in the task at hand. She would know him to be a man of amiable good cheer, a pleasant companion, a man of ready intelligence. He would discover in her a woman of sturdy emotion, with a sly appreciation of his finer qualities, a woman adaptable to adventure without being excessively enthusiastic. She and Aaron would get along quite nicely. They would become acquainted. They would emerge good friends, having arrived in those few moments or more, at a mutual appreciation that might have taken time untold to achieve under less singular circumstances.

Aaron had already reversed the position of Declan Tovey. His shoes were three steps down, and the jacket, shirt and pants were turned around so the man seemed to be lying on the stones, landing, and steps, rather than having fallen backward, unable to arise and to right himself. What remained was to stick each separate bone into place within the clothing, making sure the femur was above the tibia and fibula in the pants leg and the humerus above the ulna and radius in the sleeve. (Not for nothing had the words and the sounds of the words fascinated him in eighth grade. What could be more exciting than to become acquainted with objects named "thoracic vertebrae," "scapula," "patella," and, best of all, "clavicle." His interest at first suggested that he should become a doctor, but when he realized that it was the sound of the words—the way they shaped themselves in the mouth and on the tongue—he knew he was destined to be a man of words, a writer, that most blessed of men, one accompanied throughout life by the rhythms and resonance, the thrusts and roundings of the world's most glorious achievement: the word.)

Now at Aaron's feet lay the familiar skeleton of Declan Tovey, reconstituted except for the placement of the skull near the closed panel, where it would declare the completion of his task. There were many questions, more than Aaron's intellect had the capacity to contain. But there was only one answer. Of this Aaron could be sure. Declan Tovey had been done in by a jealous hand. Who might have struck the blow or poured the poison was still a mystery, but one that seemed susceptible to resolution by even the most inept corps of police. What stood in the way, implacably, was the resistance in these parts to easy clarifications. Indifference to the simple seemed indigenous, the insistence on complexity congenital, and the reach for widening involvement gleefully encouraged. With each of the accused accusing another, the roster of suspects could lengthen indefinitely. The entire town could be drawn into the affair, each fingering the other, a reign of suspicion, until the entire weave of the communal fabric was reduced to rags and tatters, the maid-pale peace turned blue in the face. Declan Tovey's bones would be dragged from pillow to post, rattling in protest, all jumbled, worn finally to a fine dust it would have taken eon upon eon for nature itself to achieve.

Just as Aaron began bending down to put the hairless skull in place on the step, completing his act of restoration, he heard a click at the top of the closed panel. The timing had been perfect. He had been given the exact number of minutes and seconds he'd needed to fulfill his rite of piety. Now the panel would open, and he could display the fruits of that piety to a surprised aunt and to an admiring Lolly McKeever. He would be given solemn thanks interspersed with questions and wonderments as to how he had done so remarkable a deed. Happy blessings would be bestowed as the bones were returned to the priest's bed, the sheet handled with the utmost care so as to preserve his handiwork and restore some semblance of respect for the desecrated remains.

Aaron stood one step below Declan's shoes, his own head just a bit higher—from the panel's perspective—than the skull. In tribute to the completion of his task, Aaron took in a deep breath.

Instantly, in defense of itself, his epiglottis slammed shut, but not before some of the fetid vapors had rushed into his throat, into his lungs, and, by some uncharted route, into his eyes and forehead. He coughed, choked, and coughed again. Tears flooded his eyes. Something was stinging the inside of his nose. His windpipe refused to open. After three great gasps some air was allowed to pass through his nose, but the coughing and the choking were beyond his control. A banging was heard. The panel swung open. Aaron lurched, stumbling, falling, rising, crawling up the steps. In the scramble Declan was sent clattering down in even greater disarray than he had suffered before. The skull, almost crushed by Aaron's knee, then kicked backward by Aaron's foot, rolled, then bounced from step to step down to what depths Aaron had no inclination to measure. He thrust the upper part of his body through the opening and laid his head on the floor, his chest heaving, his mouth panting, his hands splayed open on the wooden boards, an attempt to secure a hold that would counter any attempt by the vile air to draw him back into its pestilential dank.

No one came to his aid. No surprised voice spoke his name, no helping hand was lowered to calm his panting frame. Through unwiped tears he saw not the sneakered foot of his aunt or the perfectly formed ankle of Lolly McKeever, but two brown-booted feet and the cuffs of a pair of black woolen pants that could only be worn by Kieran Sweeney. Aaron braced his hands on the floorboards and three times raised his upper torso, taking in first the belted girth of Kieran, second the skirt of his aunt and the jeans of Lolly, and third the movement of Kieran past him toward the panel opening.

Aaron used his fourth and final pushup to pull the rest of himself through the panel and drag himself closer to the sneakers of his aunt, who, in turn, moved away toward the spindly table and the crucifix. He considered putting himself at the feet of Lolly

McKeever, but, suspecting that his aunt had been repelled by the tunnel odor that must have seeped from his clothes and into his flesh, he twisted his body around and sat up. Kieran was standing at the opened panel, one hand resting on the wall above the wainscoting. His head was bowed, his face relaxed and passive as if his thoughts were leading him so far from himself that he had become indifferent to whatever expression might take possession of his lips and chin, his eyes and his forehead.

Lolly was leaning against the doorjamb, her arms folded across her chest, her head turning slowly from Kitty to Kieran, from Kieran to Kitty, then back to Kieran again. His aunt, standing stiff and straight near the table, was looking only at Kieran. Her head she held high, her gaze immobile and hard, as if she had come to a long-sought satisfaction and was allowing it time to spread throughout her mind and signal to her blood that a particular fulfillment was at last accomplished. Aaron decided to stay where he was. So he wouldn't seem to be mocking Lolly in the Ping-Pong movements of her head from Kitty to Kieran, he looked only at his aunt. "What's going on?" he asked.

Staring at Sweeney, Kitty, in dry hard tones said, "I watched you and did nothing. When you took the nail from the crucified hand, when I saw that you knew where it was and knew what it could do, I let you condemn yourself. This is why we've hated the Sweeneys for all these years, for all these generations, and known them to be less than dust. We'd forgotten what they'd done, with nothing to remind us except our loathing and our scorn. It was the Sweeneys, then, that discovered the tunnel and knew the ways to open the wall. It was the Sweeneys that betrayed the priests for the king's gold and sent them to be hanged. It's a hangman's hand you have, Kieran Sweeney, and I'll thank you to take it from the holy wall."

Both Aaron and Lolly had been looking not at Kitty as she spoke but at Kieran who had stood unmoving, the cursed hand still resting above the dark opening in the wainscoting. Without the slightest shift in his stance, Kieran himself now chose to speak. "It was a Sweeney who was the priest and a McCloud his betrayer. Lured here by the promise of safe passage, led down these depths to the waiting English, he was delivered into the hangman's hand. And it was a McCloud did it—for gold or for silver was never said. Small wonder you've forgotten, and who will blame you? The wrath is mine and it's on your head it should be heaped."

Kitty hadn't even bothered to blink as she listened to the words, but a slight tightening of the muscles in her face made her seem more implacable. "A Sweeney truth is a proved lie. And if a Sweeney priest was handed over, how did you, the latest of this bloodied breed, know the escape was there and how it was opened? Can you answer me that?"

"A foolish question, and the answer is obvious. Did no brother or sister, no father or no mother come to say good-bye and watch him pass through to his death?"

Kitty's lips twitched to stop a smile. Her eyes narrowed only slightly and, without any motion whatsoever, she seemed to have raised her head even higher, "Yes, they came to say good-bye and see all the secrets of the house. But the priest was safely gone and not betrayed, and the brothers and the sisters, the father and the mother, used their knowing to sell others to their deaths."

"And I'm here to tell you otherwise."

Aaron wanted to get up or at least to shift his weight. He was still sitting on the floor, his left leg twisted under his right, his left arm braced on the floor, taking the full burden of his upper body. The flashlight was half under his left buttock, the light still on, the beam heading straight for Lolly's shoes. His arm ached, his buttock was becoming numb, and a crick had settled into his neck, the pain advancing toward his forehead. But he was, he knew, forbidden to move. The tableau could not be broken until all the speeches had been spoken. Only a change in topic could release him. And since the dialogue was given over entirely to an exchange of accusation and counteraccusation, he knew it would probably continue for quite some time. The silence of centuries had been broken, and, more likely than not, yet another century must be dedicated to making up for lost time. The two contenders, now engaged in open combat, had no choice but to prolong the fight until exhaustion was the only available mercy to end the exchange. And that either his aunt or Kieran Sweeney might be susceptible to exhaustion, given the stamina sustained by a centuries-old quarrel, was one possibility that Aaron knew better than to entertain. He was witness to one of the more perverse wooings ever enacted in human history.

Aaron was able to assure himself that the truth would never be known, not just because it was unthinkable, but because it was very much beside the point. How Sweeney knew what he knew, how Kitty surmised what she surmised, who had been betrayed by whom, was less than secondary to the emotional life being engendered by the quarrel itself. Seldom had Aaron seen such restrained passion, the heat pretending to be cold, longing disguised as scorn, yearning as contempt, and the protestation of loathing a plea to see it for the lust it truly was.

But Kitty was staring only at Kieran's back, and Kieran was staring only into the opening, and the next phase of courtship seemed far off in an unseeable future. Aaron despaired when he heard his aunt say, "But the seawall was never broken. The captors were never let know the tunnel's end. The priest was delivered not at the foot of the cliff but down the beach, away from the secret place, and no questions asked."

His despair increased when Kieran, his voice still without modulation, said, "It was the McClouds that made sure the captors never knew the tunnel was there, or the opening onto the sea. It was the McClouds that led the hapless priest, sold and delivered up———"

Lolly brought the scene to an end. She had crossed one ankle over the other, the tip of her shoe touching the floor in a somewhat pleasing fashion. This was the first movement to be made in the room since Aaron had sat up. "Can't we get Declan out of that miserable place?" she said. "He was no priest, and he doesn't belong there to begin with. Come on now. Who's for Declan Tovey?" She advanced toward the wall and knocked Sweeney's hand away so that he had to take a step back to keep from falling into the opening.

Aaron was halfway up when he realized that he had become ossified in the pose to which he'd been condemned. He paused for not more than a second, then continued his rise, rejoicing in the pain that was the price of freedom. "I'll go first," he said. "I have the flashlight." Sweeney had stepped aside, and Aaron ducked down to make his second entry of the day into the dark dank.

"I'm with you," said Lolly.

Declan Tovey was delivered from this latest tomb, bone by bone, handed through to Sweeney and to Kitty. The steps had not increased in width since Aaron's previous experience. He and Lolly brushed and knocked against each other frequently. This inspired Aaron to say, "I wonder how far down it goes."

"All the way," was Lolly's answer.

"Maybe we could explore."

"Hand me that hand. And go find the other."

As the last of the clutter was being passed through and then the sheet, Aaron said, "The skull went down the steps. You want to help me find it?"

"You've got the light. You find it." She stooped and went back into the room.

The skull was found, chipped on the forehead. An attempt was made to set Declan Tovey to rights yet again on the priest's bed. Aaron had broken one of the legs and three ribs in his thoughtless lunge when the panel had opened. The knuckle of a left forefinger seemed lost for good. Aaron was universally abused for his treatment of the dead man's bones, with Lolly the loudest.

When the criticisms reached their highest pitch—it was then that Aaron resolved to discover the murderer, his one sure way of revenge, of punishing at least one of the three ingrates bending over the bed, grabbing Tovey's bones from one another, correcting one another's presumed errors three times over, making of the thatcher a misshapen grotesque.

No sooner had this foul resolve steeled itself within Aaron's soul than a car screeched into the side yard and pulled up alongside Sweeney's truck. Two *gardaí* got out, slammed the car doors shut with punitive swings of the arm, and started toward the kitchen door.

8

Even the most convenient coincidence can be thwarted by the uncooperative act of one of its participants. In this instance everyone but Aaron conspired to keep the police at bay until Declan, again, could be disposed of in whatever manner might suggest itself at the moment. So flurried was the activity as the police came closer to the kitchen door that before Aaron was completely aware, he and Lolly were left alone with Declan, sworn to protect him from capture.

It had been Aaron's intention to invite the police in, confront them with the bundled remains, and have the matter ended once and for all. That he would betray, perhaps, his aunt or Lolly or even Sweeney, who'd saved his life, would not be allowed to quench his thirst for justice. They had exasperated him. They had treated him badly. They had taken advantage of his good nature. They had given him no credit for his reverent treatment of their friend. Each charge was, to him, a hanging offense, and the accumulation was more than enough to let fall the blindfold from the eyes of justice and bid her unsheathe her terrible swift sword. Then, too, he had, on their behalf, become suffused with stink and choked with vapors. He had been exposed to pestilence, and of more immediate concern, there were—he was convinced—at this moment unassailable fungi lodged between his toes, already producing yeasts and molds that would forever disqualify his feet from whatever attentions some future acquaintance, in her rapture, might feel stimulated to bestow. Mercy was obviously out of the question. Justice must take its course, channeled through the depths of his pique and prodded by the nobility of his resentments.

But he was robbed of his petty pleasures by the general confusion. The panel had been slammed shut, the door to the priest's room had been closed with Aaron and Lolly inside, greetings were being exchanged between Kitty and the police in the kitchen, invitations to search the house for an escapee had been extended— the escapee a man who'd been arrested for biting his girlfriend's gerbil to death, his abandoned bicycle found in the thicket just down the road—and, as before with Sweeney, the sound of boots now thumped overhead.

Aaron let Lolly go through the prescribed banging for reopening the wall. After two bangs she admitted that she didn't remember the actual place. Aaron pretended to try, surprised that Lolly's desperation had effected a change in attitude. She was helpless; she was trapped; she was dependent on him for rescue. If proof were needed that it was in her interest that the skeleton not be found, it was being acted out before him now, complete with repetitions of the word "shit," wringing of hands, and widening of eyes—restored in her plight to their deepest blue—a plea that she not be handed over to the brutes slamming and banging walls over their heads. The boot steps were in the upstairs hall. They were nearing the stairs. A closed door—the door to the priest's room—would get their first attention when they came down.

"Oh, Declan," Lolly said, "you were always trouble. And look at you now."

Aaron had no choice; he must come to her aid. She was in trouble. She needed him. In what was perhaps the most futile attempt possible, Aaron went to the window and tried to pry open the shutters. Maybe they could dump the remains outside, then retrieve them before the police searched the grounds.

But now the boots were clomping down the stairs. Kitty, seldom the gracious hostess, was laughing. His fingertips unable to penetrate the slit between the shutters, Aaron almost hit his fist against the wood in frustration, but was stopped by the sound of a click behind him. The adventure was at an end. Justice was no farther than the door. The police would now invade, Declan would be discovered, there would be amazements, questions, stammerings, further amazements, and then some action as yet unimagined. Whether anyone other than Declan would be hauled away was as yet unknown. What accusations would be made, what alibis given, what protestations made, he had not the slightest notion. Aaron's only surmise was that there would be unending babble, with only Declan excused from making a contribution. And then—with a clarity available only to his inner eye—the confusion came to an end. Lolly McKeever, in plain tones, would confess to the crime. No one would move. No one would speak. Someone would weep. He suspected it would be himself.

Aaron turned away from the shuttered window, prepared to accept any and all eventualities. But the door had been opened only slightly, and Lolly had put her face in the crack. She had unbuttoned the top of her blouse and was clutching it closed with her hand. She had slipped out of her shoes and had disheveled her hair.

"Please," she whispered. "You can give us just a bit more time. Give him a chance at least to make himself decent."

A voice gruff with embarrassment answered. "The escaped

man's bike was found just down the road on the other side of the wall. And it's known there's a secret room someplace in this house———"

Kitty's laugh came again. "An old tale—and do you believe it?"

"Believe it or not, the man could be hiding and you wouldn't know it. But we'll find him. You'll see."

Lolly clutched the top of her blouse closer to her throat. "Look to the other rooms like the good friends you are, Tom McTygue, and you, Jim Collins. Then come back, can't you? I'm shamed enough, but I'd be that much more shamed if you saw him the way he is now, to say nothing of myself."

"Lolly McKeever? You?" said a hoarse voice.

"Please, Tom. Please, Jim. Only a moment I ask, here as I am, in the depths of my embarrassment. And you have my promise: There are no gerbil killers here. Promise."

"Well, then. Pull yourselves together. Pull yourselves together. And we'll do our job and be gone."

Lolly nodded her head, drew back from the door, and quickly closed it. She rushed back to the bed, yanked up the sheet by the two corners on the far side of the bed, then the two corners on her side. The clothes folded down inside, the bones—not for the first time—were clacked one against the other. "Lift the mattress," she whispered. "Quick, you stupid lump."

Aaron lifted the mattress. Lolly placed the sheet over the wide slats and spread it open. With a haste that disregarded the courtesy due to the dead, she distributed the bones as evenly as she could, taking time only to put the cap over the skull as if protecting the face from what was to happen next. "Put back the mattress. Put it back." Aaron put the mattress back, on top of the bones. Lolly rumpled the blanket even more than it had been already. She then punched into the pillow an even deeper hollow than Declan's skull had made. That accomplished, she sat down on the edge of the bed. Aaron thought he heard a bone snap. He closed his eyes, hoping to deafen himself.

"Sit here. Next to me. Look sheepish," she hissed. She unbuttoned one more button on her blouse, gave her hair a good scrub with the tips of her fingers, put her hands on her lap, and bowed her head. Aaron sat next to her. He heard a crunching sound. "Your shirt looks just right with all the buttons popped away," she rasped out from the side of her mouth. "And here, hold my hand like we don't give a damn." She joined their hands and thumped them down on his thigh, more a punch than a tender touch. "Lower your head. I'll be the bold one."

There was a light tap at the door. "Yes, Tom. Yes, Jim," she said quietly, giving Aaron's hand a quick squeeze. The door opened slowly. Lolly raised her chin a bit, then, against her original intent, lowered her head, and stared down into her lap. "Aaron," she said, "this is Tom." Tom came just inside the door. "Tom, this is Aaron, Kitty's nephew and a friend from when we were children." Tom nodded. "And Aaron, this is Jim." Jim entered, placing himself in front of Tom. "Jim, this is Aaron. From America."

Jim did not nod. "You're from America?"

"New York," Aaron corrected.

Jim, too, nodded, as if Aaron had clarified everything. Lolly pressed their clasped hands deeper into Aaron's thigh. "We're to be married," she said. "Aaron's my fiancé. As you must have guessed from the two of us here like this. That's why he's here. From New York."

For Aaron there seemed no reason to alter the stupid look he'd already taken on, but when Lolly kissed his cheek he felt he should make some acknowledgment of this sudden thrust toward possibility. He lifted his head and smiled, hoping the smile didn't present itself as a leer.

"Married, then," said Jim.

"Engaged," said Tom, stepping in front of Jim. "Kitty's nephew. From New York."

Aaron nodded, then assumed again his stupid look, which consisted mostly of a stare too befuddled to be blank and too aghast to hint of contentment. He was, of course, honored by this sudden election, until he reminded himself that this was a betrothal of convenience. Lolly would break the engagement once Officer Tom and Officer Jim had completed their mission and vacated the priestly room. In the meantime he would hold the woman's hand, keep his head down, and not even try to anticipate what might lie ahead. In the murder he was now an accessory after the fact.

By this time Kitty and Sweeney had sidled into the room and edged toward the wall near the secret opening. Both of them, pretending to relieve a crick in the neck, looked around the room, glancing under the bed, staring at the ceiling, trying to detect the whereabouts of their departed friend. Awed by his absence, they inched even closer to the panel. Then Kitty spoke up, her voice coated with the honey produced only in the throats of those expressing the end of patience by pointedly pretending a civility completely foreign to their basic natures. "Are there any escaped prisoners present? Do you see anyone who has bitten a gerbil? If not, perhaps you gentlemen would like to continue your search elsewhere."

Immediately Jim turned to face her as if wondering where the voice had come from. "Doing our job," he said. Tom, who'd been unable to take his eyes from the happy couple seated on the bed, finally gave a quick look around the room. Instinctively both Aaron and Lolly spread their legs a little, hoping to obscure whatever parts or pieces of Declan might be sticking out and to discourage these guardians of the peace from looking under the bed. The movement, however, drew Tom's attention, and he, re-

sponding to instincts of his own, stooped down and looked
under the bed. So as not to obstruct the law, Aaron and Lolly, resigned to whatever might happen, not only drew their legs together but pressed them closer to each other's, his to hers, hers
to his. Tom stood up. Lolly's leg started to make the slightest
movement away, then stayed where it was, pressing just a little
bit closer.

Jim had busied himself opening and closing the cupboard
door, taking his own obligatory peek under the bed, then thump-
ing up and down on the floorboards, one boot at a time. Tom
poked at the ceiling with a stick that had materialized in his hand.
He nodded in brief reverence when he passed the crucifix, then
checked the cupboard again. More thorough than his partner, he
knocked with his knuckles on the inside walls of the cupboard and
tested the efficiency of the hinges on its door. The sight of Tom
pounding on the interior of the cupboard inspired Jim to hit his
fist on the wall just to the side of the bed. Not really listening for
any resonance that might suggest a hollowed space behind, he
continued his banging, his fist obviously enthusiastic about its
connection with the wall, with the wainscoting.

Kitty was the first to see the pin, the nail from the crucifix,
still sticking out from the wall where Sweeney had placed it.
Aaron noticed the quick jerk of his aunt's head, followed her gaze,
and saw the nail. Jim continued his banging, now joined by Tom,
the two of them equally eager to demonstrate how thorough they
were in the fulfillment of their duty.

It was Jim who hit his fist in the proper place. The panel door
creaked open, forcing Kitty and Sweeney to step away. Ever adaptable, Lolly cried out, "Look! A secret panel!"

"Jesus, Mary, and Joseph," said Tom.

Jim gagged, then said, "What's that smell? Old cabbages?"

Tom put his hand to his chin. Jim covered his mouth and

made an inhuman sound. Kitty and Sweeney leaned backward to further demonstrate their amazement even as Lolly pressed her thigh closer to Aaron's, drew their clasped hands up to her lips, and give a quick gnaw to one of Aaron's knuckles.

"Come out! And don't be making us wait!" Tom yelled.

Jim shouted even more loudly. "We've got you now. So save yourself and come along like a good fellow!" He waved his hand to indicate he meant what he said.

Tom, without turning away from the opening, said from the side of his mouth, the side closest to Kitty, "Where does it go? Is there another way out?"

"I wouldn't know. I've never seen it before in my life."

"There's the old story that there's a tunnel leading to the sea," said Jim. "This is it. And we've found it."

"Imagine that," said Kitty.

"Come out!" Tom called again.

"There's no one there," said Sweeney. "Only an idiot would put foot into a stench like that."

Aaron started to raise his head in protest, but decided not to speak up on his own behalf. Lolly had replaced their joined hands on his thigh and had relaxed her spine to indicate that the police were on the wrong track. Kitty picked up on the signal. She took the flashlight from the dresser and said, "Come on. I'll go first. If anyone's there, it'll be a ghost, and I'd like to see who it is."

Tom and Jim exchanged glances. Kitty bent down, ready to enter the tunnel. "But," said Sweeney, trying not to wring his hands—not having seen Lolly's signal—"are you sure you want to do this? I mean, you can't tell what might be in there. Please. Think."

Without straightening, Kitty said, "Whatever might be there is there. I just want to get it over with and get on with my career." She flicked the flashlight on and beamed it into the dark.

Lolly took in a breath, exhaled, then said, "You won't find anything. I can promise you that."

"Oh?" said Tom.

"You sound so terribly sure," said Jim. How is that?"

Lolly shrugged. "I just know, is all." She looked straight at Sweeney. Sweeney returned her gaze, then turned toward the still-stooped Kitty. "I'll go in," he said. "It's no place for a woman, whatever's there or not there." At the sound of his voice, Tom and Jim, like stagehands slightly behind in their cues with the spotlights, turned their eyes on Sweeney. "We'll be the ones to go," said Jim, "if anyone goes at all." Kitty, with a snort, entered the opening.

After the eyes of Tom consulted with the eyes of Jim, the two men stooped down, prepared to follow. Jim stuck his head inside, withdrew it, spit, then entered. Tom entered next, tripping. Out of the dark came the single sound, "Ouch," in Jim's voice.

Lolly quickly unclasped her hand from Aaron's and flicked it three times as if to rid it of his touch. Her thigh was separated from his, and with nimble fingers she began to button her blouse. "And I've got hogs waiting for me," she said. She got up and went to the opening. Aaron followed. The two of them looked down, listening for the sounds to recede. Twice came Jim's "Ogh" and once Tom's "Don't shove" and, now in the distance, Kitty's "Let me know when you gentlemen are satisfied."

Sweeney went to the bed and, lowering himself onto the mattress, whispered, "What did you do with Declan?" There was a cracking, then a crunching as he sat a few inches lower onto the mattress. Lolly and Aaron turned to look.

"Oh," said Sweeney.

"Sweeney," said Lolly. "Get up before you do him more damage than you've done already. And you, Aaron, help me get him out before they all come back."

"Out?" said Aaron.

"We'll bundle him up, and I'll straighten him out at home."

"You're going to take him with you?"

"We can't leave him here."

Sweeney put his opened palms at his sides, resting on the mattress. "I'm the one came to take him. He'll go with me."

Aaron considered calling down to Tom and Jim, telling them to come quick, he had something to show them. Anything to stop the bickering. And besides, Lolly's need for him had exhausted itself. And he had very little doubt that Lolly McKeever was the killer. Her frantic need to hide the skeleton was as close to a confession as anyone would want. And then her blatant use of him, of Aaron, while not without its moments, was, in retrospect, shameless, without scruple and, worst of all, insincere. He knew that the clasp of her hand, the pressure of her thigh, and the gnaw of his knuckle had been inspired bits of acting, but so convincing had they been that he had begun to believe that she had, in her distress, come to realize the attractions of his nearness, the irresistible reality of his hand, his thigh, his knuckle. But she had moved too quickly from his side, from the hold of his hand and the touch of his thigh. He knew himself reduced to what she considered him: a necessary but temporary prop. He didn't ask her gratitude. He wanted only some sizable acknowledgment that she had been aroused by his proximity. A bit of perplexity on her part was all he required, an embarrassed indication that she had been moved beyond the usual controls, a halting plea that she be allowed to pull herself together after what she had experienced in his presence.

Sweeney sucked in a quick breath and said in a desperate whisper, "The pig is in the grave!" Wildly waving his arms, he left the room, knocking against the doorframe as he passed through.

Once across the hall, he repeated the same injury on the doorway into the kitchen and yet again on the door leading out to the yard. The screen door slammed, and through the screen Aaron could see Sweeney, like a demented dancer, rushing toward the hole where Declan had been laid. The top of the pig was visible, the pink mound slipping from side to side. Even to a city boy like Aaron, it was evident that the pig had created for itself a wallow, rooting down far enough to wet the bottom of the grave, and was now enjoying the fruits of its labor. If Aaron heard right, Sweeney was making hissing sounds more appropriate to a goose than to a pig. He was now circling the grave, the pink mound slipping back and forth even more excitedly, the pig driven to a greater gratification by the shamanistic dancing of the man with the flapping hands and the inspired boots.

As if to prevent either Aaron or Lolly from interfering, or even observing this primitive rite, a sudden gust from somewhere slammed shut the door to the priest's room. Aaron was near the door. Lolly was near the bed. They were alone.

Both remained still, suspended between what had been happening and what would happen now. When Aaron made no move, Lolly, to suggest that motion was allowed, went back to the bed and sat down. There was the crunch, but she paid no attention. She put her hands on her lap and stared at the closed door. Aaron, after a moment, went to the chair next to the cabinet and sat down. He put one hand on each thigh and stared at the panel opening. No movement was made for about a minute. Then Lolly got up and went to the shuttered window. After running the tips of her fingers along the line where the shutters met the sill, she gave a slight pull and the shutter came toward her. She repeated the action and the second shutter was drawn into the room. Next she put a little pressure on the window frame and raised it from

the bottom. She stood a moment staring blankly at the scene outside, then went and sat stiffly on the severe Protestant bench and
gazed out the window.

A soft breeze rippled into the room, bringing with it the scent
of apples even though this was far from their season. From where
he sat Aaron could see a broad field of tall grass bending toward
the sea, an impossibility since all winds came from the west.
Rather than take up this latest addition to his bewilderment, he
simply remarked to himself—actually something closer to a sigh
than a remark—how graceful the grass was in its submission to
the winds. There was a lone tree he knew to be an oak. Often they
had picnicked in its shade before time and the sea had moved it so
perilously close to the edge of the cliff. Rising in the distance was
a wide band of water separating the land's end and the sky's beginning. Only a single boat could be seen, a curragh, and even that
could be the crest of a wave that seemed wary of coming closer to
the shore. Great masses of snow white cloud, like venerable kingdoms arising in majesty from the sea, sat unmoving in the sky to
the north, certain that they had found their rightful place in the
cosmos and would remain where they were until kingdoms were
no more. The wind stirred the leaves of the oak, but the grass refused to bend more than it already had. Near the horizon the boat
had disappeared, either a wave that had crested and crashed or the
boat itself sunk and gone.

"Will you stay long enough to see the foxglove?" Lolly asked
quietly. "And the wild dog rose should come before too long. You
should see that too." She was smiling, her eyelids slightly lowered,
as if seeing already the flowers whose season had not yet come.
When Aaron didn't answer, she looked toward him, eyes wide,
still smiling softly. "Of course now you get the buttercup and the
stitchwort, and they're lovely, I know; but it's the foxglove you
should see."

"Yes," said Aaron. "I'd like to. But I'm not really sure how long I'll stay."

"You've come so far. You shouldn't leave too soon." Her smile had saddened, sorry for what might be lost to him. And her voice had become almost gentle. Aaron looked out through the window. A tiny brown bird was dipping into the grass, in and out, up and down, as if looking for something it had left behind. "What bird is that?"

"That? A reed bunting. Silly bird. Prefers telephone wires to just about anything else."

"It's having a fine time now, in the grass."

"Probably has a nest and forgot, poor thing."

"How sad not to know the names of birds."

"But some you know."

"Some. Not many."

"Do you have a favorite?"

"I never thought of it. Maybe."

"Which one?"

"The ones I've never seen. Like a bluebird or a nightingale or an eagle."

"You've never seen an eagle?"

"No. Never."

"How strange. You really must."

"Yes." Aaron gave a quick smile, then looked again out the window. "My favorite, I think, is the cormorant. Except I saw one, here, yesterday, a cormorant near the cliffs."

"Your favorite?" She was more puzzled than surprised. "A greedy thing like that?"

"The sound. 'Cormorant.' I loved the sound even as a boy, the way it works the mouth just to say it. 'Cormorant.'"

"There's one now," Lolly said, nodding toward the window.

There, as if summoned, winging its way out over the cliffs,

riding the air, wings spread wide as if in ecstasy, was the scorned scavenger, indifferent to the world's contempt. "Yes. A cormorant. I'd forgotten it was my favorite." The bird plunged down below the cliff, then suddenly rose up again as if it had landed on a tarp and been sent bouncing back into view. Off it soared to the south, satisfied that it had completed the demonstration the mention of its name had required.

"Cormorant," Lolly said.

"Yes. Fine word. No matter what."

"Yes. A fine word. I'll remember that." Again she was smiling her inward smile, anticipating a future time when the word would come to her mind and she would say it half out loud and remember the moment when this new appreciation had come to her. Aaron watched as the smile slowly relaxed and Lolly returned to contemplating the hands folded on her lap.

He listened for any sounds that might come from the panel opening. Was the tunnel really a labyrinth and were they lost? *Had* someone been hidden there? He listened more closely, heard nothing except the twittering of yet another bird he could not name. The calm was welcome, and the ease of Lolly's quiet company was too natural for him to be surprised. He watched her hands as she recrossed her thumb, lengthened an index finger, then curled it in again, closer to the thumb. He took note of her breasts. Relaxed and ample, they seemed comfortable, neither demanding nor defiant. His gaze must have lingered longer than he'd thought. When he lifted his eyes, he saw that Lolly was smiling at him. Aaron, too, smiled, warmed by the thought that she in turn had noted his attention and was now acknowledging it as an acceptable act, expected even, requiring no further comment or gesture from either of them.

To reciprocate she seemed now to be considering either his nose or his ears, he couldn't be sure. In reflex he blinked his eyes, preferring that these be the focus of her regard. Having duly become aware that it was his face that interested her— it seemed, finally, his ears—she leaned forward toward the opened wainscoting, not impatient, merely checking—as Aaron had done. Still nothing could be heard. She leaned back again and seemed about to rest her head against the wall but obviously decided instead to simply gaze not toward Aaron but out the window she had so effortlessly opened.

In response another breeze wafted into the room, this time smelling more of manure than of apples—even though there were no cattle near, any more than apples were stored out under the eaves. Aaron looked down at his khaki shorts, at his shirt, at his squished feet. Had the breeze, in passing him, brought his own scent into his nostrils? He had forgotten that the deposit from his swim and the seeped stench of the tunnel had become the very fabric of his clothes, permeating at the same time his pores even unto the hair follicles of his head, chest, arms, legs and elsewhere too. That it was merely manure that could be smelled might be to his advantage.

"My pigs must miss me," Lolly said, her voice seemed sad for the sorrows of her swine. Aaron, without effort, could guess at what had put the thought into her head. He nodded but didn't look up. "Mine are the only pigs that smell like bran," she said. "And I don't feed them bran. But that's what they smell like. Bran." Again Aaron nodded. "They must be missing me." Again her voice was sad, but amused at its own sadness.

Aaron decided not to nod. She might be bored by the repetition. Instead he said, "I never liked cabbage until I was fourteen. Then I liked it."

Now it was Lolly who nodded. She waited a moment, then said, "Come sometime, see the pigs. Then you'll know. Like bran they smell."

Before Aaron could take yet another turn nodding, a definite murmur came through the opened wall. As the sound came closer, it grew to a mutter, a collective mutter, then to the almost distinguishable voices of several people—three to be exact—caught in, of course, a quarrel. No particular word was able to rise above the rest, but not for want of trying. Finally, as the sound came closer, "finger" could be made out, possibly in Jim's voice, then "believe" in Tom's, then "breathe" in Kitty's. The garbling came nearer. "Shine the light," followed by, "Keep walking," followed by, "Is it what I think it is?" followed by, "I can't breathe, and you want to start collecting souvenirs." Then, at the last, "But it's a piece of bone. I can feel it's a bone!"

"Part of Declan's finger," Aaron murmured. "They've found it." The beam of the flashlight hit the ceiling, crossed to the far side, and, as the ascent was made up the tunnel steps, the light began its descent along the far wall. Lolly got up and quickly smoothed the blanket on the bed, running her hand along the edge of the mattress to make sure Declan was safely stowed beneath. She shook out her hair as if not quite sure of what might have happened or what might have been said since she had been left alone with Aaron in the room.

Kitty's head poked through the opening, preceded by the beam of the flashlight made pale by the light from the opened window. Before she could make it through the panel, she was shoved aside by Jim, who stumbled into the room and rushed to the window. He held up what seemed like a trinket, turning it over and over to see what refractions might be caught in the light. "It *is* a bone! Like a knucklebone," he said. Kitty made it into the room, followed by Tom. Kitty brushed the hair from her forehead and rubbed the flashlight along her cheek. "What's that awful smell?" she asked.

Tom joined Jim at the window, the two of them regarding

with awe what was obviously the found knucklebone of Declan Tovey. Tom tried to take it from Jim's hand, but Jim pulled it out of reach, waited for Tom to lower his arm, then held the bone up to the light once more. "A relic," Jim whispered. "A holy relic. Some martyred priest. The blessings I'll get."

"It's a fish bone," Tom said.

"Because you didn't find it."

"It's still a fish bone."

"You have no faith."

"I have no faith in fish bones, if that's what you mean."

The screen door slammed. Sweeney burst into the room, the flung door slamming Kitty against the wall. "The pig," he gasped. "The pig is in the grave!"

For want of a more original response, both Lolly and Aaron stiffened, and possibly Kitty too, still stuck as she was between the door and the wall. Sweeney seemed to have immediately realized the error of his announcement and, scratching his chest, wetting his lips, managed to say, "I mean———" But before be could complete his revision, Jim, gaining heat from Tom's heresies, dangled the bone in front of his colleague's face. "We'll see what Father Colavin has to say. I'm showing it to him and telling him the whole story and then we'll see . . ." He stopped and turned slowly to look at Sweeney. Tom, too, turned his head, but even more slowly.

"What pig?" asked Jim.

"And a grave?" asked Tom.

"No, no, nothing. No pig. No grave," Sweeney answered.

"Didn't you just say, 'The pig is in the grave'?"

"Oh. That. Yes. Yes, I did say that."

Jim closed his fist over the bone as if to protect it from whatever disrespect might come from talk about a pig. "Then I'm asking again, what pig?"

"Yes," Tom said, unwilling to yield his proprietary rights to the question that had been of his own devising. "What grave?"

Kitty slid out from behind the door, rubbing a shoulder. "His name is Sweeney. You know that. So why do you listen to one word he says? They never know what they're talking about. A bunch of blatherers if ever there was one, almost always muttering about pigs and graves and sheep and shrouds. And you're paying him the least attention? You must be as idiot as he."

"Idiot, am I?" Sweeney drew himself up at least another quarter of an inch.

"If you're a Sweeney, the word applies. And enough of pigs and graves and whatever madness has come over you."

Sweeney managed to find, somewhere in either his spine or his neck, enough slack to raise his height yet one more quarter inch. "These men know better than to listen to slander. In their profession they know that only the truth is of interest. The facts, no more. And they also know, as does the entire civilized population, that to be a Sweeney is also to be a poet. And if you can't recognize poetry when you hear it, you don't belong to the land where you were born. It was a poem I was reciting. 'The pig is in the grave.' Have you never heard of symbolism? Is metaphor an area of ignorance? Listen then, will you? 'The pig is in the grave.' Can you hear it now? Have you or have you not an ear for cadence?" He shifted his proud gaze from Kitty to Jim and Tom. "*You* can hear it, can't you? *You* know poetry when it's visited upon you. 'The pig is in the grave.' Ponder, gentlemen. Ponder. And then admit to me and to all gathered here that you are in the presence of a poet."

Lolly and Aaron allowed themselves to slump slightly. Jim looked for another moment at Sweeney, thinking, then turned back to the light coming in through the window. Again he held up the relic. Tom continued to regard Sweeney, thought requiring for him a bit more time. Then he, too, returned his attentions to the bone. "Superstitious nonsense."

"Faith," said Jim. "I'll take it to Father Colavin."

"Take it to forensics," Tom said. "They'll test it. They'll tell you the foolishness you're worshipping."

Aaron looked at Kitty, Kitty at Sweeney, Sweeney at Lolly and Lolly at Aaron. No one spoke. No one moved.

"Forensics!" Jim spit out the word. "They'll never touch it with their gloved hands, their carbon dating, and DNA and all. It's faith tells all we need to know."

"All we need to know about fish bones. Fish bones and faith."

Kitty relaxed first, then Lolly, then Sweeney, then Aaron. Lolly, at her most casual, said, "Aren't you supposed to be looking for an escaped prisoner?"

"We are looking, thank you very much," Jim said. "And we'll continue looking, if you'll excuse us. Come, Tom. We'll go to Father Colavin. And you'll be begging indulgences from what I hold in my hand before the day is out. And you'll be given nothing back but your own scorn."

Their shoes weighted with the full authority of their calling, Jim and Tom stomped out the door, across the hall, through the kitchen, and out into the yard. Aaron could see them pause for only the briefest moment when they saw the pig wallowing down in the hole, allowing, no doubt, some fleeting thought to pass through their minds. As they continued toward the car, Tom alone looked back, his head turning slowly. He faced front abruptly when he bumped into the back fender of their car.

Aaron, Lolly, Kitty and Sweeney watched silently as the car drove away, Declan's knucklebone no doubt laid out on the dashboard, guarding against all evil in this world and the next.

After the car had driven out of sight, Aaron, Lolly, Kitty and Sweeney turned as one and looked toward the bed where the rest of Declan Tovey lay smothered and crunched beneath the flimsy mattress known heretofore only to priests.

"I think," said Kitty, "that before we do anything more or say anything more, we all have a bit of a drink."

9

inally everything was settled. Aaron felt that the combatants, himself included, succumbed at the last to exhaustion and to the fellow feeling of having shared and survived a somewhat energetic day. Then, too, the Tullamore Dew they were drinking may well have made its contribution to the newly generated amity. Assignments were made. Assignments were accepted. Aaron would enlarge and deepen the grave, Sweeney would make the coffin, and Kitty and Lolly would do the women's work of preparing the corpse.

Sweeney's brother would milk his cows, Lolly's sister would tend her pigs, Kitty's novel would be given a time of rest, and Aaron's suffering would be—yet one more time—postponed. And so they set themselves to work.

When Aaron started out to dig a more commodious grave, Sweeney was already, with a crowbar, taking down some of Kitty's bookshelves, the books themselves candidates for corrections— from Elizabeth Bowen to Virginia Woolf, with, ominously, a new section devoted to Joyce Carol Oates. The oak would make a worthy coffin. To purchase boards in town would inevitably lead to unwanted questions, and Sweeney was a man loath to lie, especially to his friend Diarmid Dunne, from whom he'd have to buy the lumber. Aaron himself had been obliged to hand over a pair of socks, some undershorts, and a clean shirt, so the women could properly prepare the skeleton. (Aaron had feared that his one good suit was about to be appropriated and his last pair of shoes as well, but the fits were wrong—Aaron's fault, they implied—and the rest of his wardrobe survived intact.)

It was during the fulfillment of these various tasks that Aaron was given some insight as to why the decision regarding immediate burial had been agreed to by each participant from the start. When he helped Sweeney remove the books from the confiscated shelves, the man leaned close to his ear and said, "Before all this is over, she'll confess. Prepare yourself. I know she's your aunt, but I know she'll let it all come out before the coffin hits the ground." Aaron had said nothing, simply continuing to remove the complete works of Aphra Behn from the shelf.

As he'd handed the shirt to his aunt upstairs in his room, she had, in tones of sturdy practicality, said, "Don't get yourself too interested in Lolly McKeever. I've consented to all this because it's the best way to get her to admit what she's done. Before the poor body is laid to rest, she'll confess." Again Aaron had said nothing, simply handing over the shirt, the socks and the undershorts.

When he'd handed Lolly the volume from the inherited *Encyclopaedia Britannica*, number 25 from the 1911 edition, so she would have something to refer to when arranging the bones—the article on skeletons—she'd accepted the book, reached over and lightly touched his arm. "I'm so happy you're here," she whispered. "You'll be a valuable witness when he confesses. And don't worry. He will. Before the bones are out of the house, he'll admit to what he's done. So pay attention." She then patted his cheek. Aaron had said nothing. He had simply reached up and touched the skin where her fingers had been, however briefly.

One last issue had yet to be resolved. It was customary for the women to wash the corpse before dressing it. There was no actual corpse to wash, but some gesture in that direction was deemed necessary. Kitty thought a simple once over with a feather duster might be enough; Lolly wanted total immersion. It was finally settled: Kitty would wash each bone with a wet cloth. Lolly would dry it with a fresh towel and place it inside the clothes. When Lolly insisted on soap, Kitty, after a moment's pause, conceded, promising as well to use the expensive and scented soap that was one of the few indulgences she allowed herself.

Aaron went outside before any more contentions could be introduced. As he headed toward the shed to get the spade, he found himself looking around for the pig. It was nowhere to be seen. Not in the garden or in the high grass leading to the cliff or across the road or even in the wallow it had so rudely made of Declan Tovey's grave. He considered looking down from the cliff to see if the animal had finally gone over the edge. But if that were so, he didn't want to see it, the pig impaled on a crag or stuck, still struggling in a crevice, or even the fat pink body plumped on the narrow beach like some sea slug washed ashore by the maddened waves.

Now that these images had passed before his inner eye, he had no choice but to go and look. He owed it to the pig. Its fate could not fulfill itself unnoted. The obsequy of a glance, a wince, a shudder, a revulsion seemed the least he could offer. He strode into the resisting grass, the pull of it at his feet as he slowly tore, more than trampled, his way toward the cliff, giving him a sense that he was being given one last chance not to proceed.

The great waves, rising high as if aghast at what they were seeing on the shore, plunged down in pity and in grief at what they were witnessing, sending heavenward the spread spray fanning out over the waters, a last gesture of despair in the face of so much that was calamitous and doomed. Surely this could not be just for the pig—if it was the pig the waves could see. Some other vision—either prophetic or present now—brought these waves to this violence, this need to destroy themselves, this determination to be spared any further sight of what lay along or beyond the shore.

Aaron stopped before he got to the cliff's edge. It was his aunt's house the waves could see, the stones gone gray with age, the slate roof blue in the bright air, the windows reflecting back the flaming flares of the lowering sun. It was Declan Tovey's grave the waves could see, the rock cairn at its head, the wind-bent trees bowing to the east, and the cluster of trucks—Sweeney's and Lolly's, along with his aunt's Acura. And they saw as well the rock wall alongside the road, the bristle and blossom of the blackberries springing out from the rocks themselves. It was Sweeney fashioning the coffin they could see, and his aunt and Lolly washing down the broken muddied bones. And it was Aaron too they saw, dragging himself through the grass toward the top of the cliff, Aaron McCloud, accessory to murder, complicitous in his every act to the death of a fellow human being, guilty in what he was doing, guilty in what he wasn't doing—he should have, either directly or by some seeming accident, revealed the bones to the *gardaí*. He should have allowed Jim to rejoin the found bone to its rightful hand and not gone off giving praise and glory. He should, with what exhausted moral and civic sense he might have left, persuaded at least one, if not all three, of his coconspirators to surrender, if not themselves, at least the hapless skeleton to the authorities, who would honor it by tracking down the perpetrator that had laid him low and given his flesh to feed the cabbages of his aunt. The wheels of justice should have been allowed to turn even if they ground to pulp his own aunt, whom he loved, or Lolly, whom he craved, or Sweeney, whom he honored. At worst he was craven; at best he was confused.

Aaron reached the end of the field. Evening had almost come.

A few clouds had paused near the horizon to give the sun some chance to make a display of itself before disappearing for the night. Rays of glory were already shooting heavenward, the orange and gold streaking the western sky suggesting in their splendor that heaven, not hell, should be a place of everlasting fire. The grass was turning damp, the air cold. The sea was ominous with warnings of the rampage it had planned once the dark had come, its vengeance on the land and on the living for the distress the daylight had visited upon it, allowing it all the sights it had seen.

The pig came snorting out of the tool shed and ambled toward the ruined garden, favoring this time what had been the beets. Aaron could now, in good if troubled conscience, get the spade and go about his criminal task.

There was water in the grave to a depth of six inches. Aaron could dig down deeper, then decide how to bail out the pig's wallow and provide Declan with a dry and suitable resting place. As he dug, thoughts of his abandonment of Phila began to surface and recede, then surface again in his consciousness. The pig, interested now in this enlargement of its handiwork, came to watch the digging. Aaron continued his labors, bringing up thick chunks of mud and placing them carefully away from the side of the grave. After a few moments he paused and looked directly at the pig.

"I've been unfaithful to Phila," he said, his voice mournful and resigned. "I try to think of her but something always happens. I want to think of her, but . . ." He stopped, sighed, and slowly shook his head. The pig blinked. "I never loved her," Aaron at last confessed. "All I wanted was for *her* to love *me*. And when she didn't, I decided to feel sorry for myself, grieving, tearing my hair, rending my garments, but it wasn't love." The pig flicked its ears but didn't move away.

"It looked like love. It felt like love. Jealousy, yearning, aching, all of it. But it wasn't love. It was obsession. I was obsessed with her. Not love. Obsession." The pig both blinked *and* flicked its ears. "There's a difference between love and obsession, even if I'm the only one knows it. She had to love me so I wouldn't have to love her. And when she didn't, I became a man obsessed. And that's the truth of it all."

The patient pig did nothing. Aaron paused a moment, considered resuming his digging, but decided instead to say just a few words more.

"Even Proust didn't know it. The difference between love and obsession. Proust thought Marcel loved Albertine. He didn't. Marcel just wanted Albertine to love him—and when she didn't, he, like me, was a man obsessed. And then, when he was convinced she *did* love him and even came to live with him, he hadn't the least idea of what to do with her now that he'd had his way. His obsession had been fulfilled, and there was nowhere to go from there. Obsession, not love." He stopped, considered this a moment, then, amazed by the realization, he looked past the tool shed, past the pasture, and out toward the sea. In tones both awed and disbelieving, he said, "I know more than Proust. Imagine. Me. More than Proust."

The pig, as at their first meeting, sent out an arc of urine from behind, as sows will do. Then, when the arc had collapsed, went back to make sure no beets had survived its repeated incursions.

Aaron returned his attention to the matter of the grave and to the water now reaching up to the top of his socks. He peeled them off, wrung them out, and tossed them toward the cairn, where one caught itself on a jagged stone near the top, hanging down like the muddied flag of a defeated leprechaun.

Aaron dug away, bringing up shovelful after shovelful of sludge that he placed far enough from the sides of the grave to prevent their return to the bottom of the hole. Not an easy job, but it gave him some sense of solidarity with the old existentialists to know that his labors were futile but that the imperatives of action demanded that he struggle with them as best he could. When a small mudslide slipped back into the grave, far from being discouraged, he accepted it as a further bonding with those masters, long superseded, with their self-dramatized resignation that excused and even glorified their ineptitude. Aaron McCloud was one with them at last—as more mud slipped and slid back into the hole.

Tom and Jim returned when Aaron was ankle deep in mud and shin deep in water. In their journey back to the station, they slowed the car to a stop to observe Aaron's labors. In the backseat was the presumed malefactor, a youth in his twenties with a high mound of black hair combed back on his head and a goatee suggesting his alliance with the devil.

Both Tom and Jim came and stood by the side of the grave. They simply stood and watched.

"And what would you be digging up?" asked Tom.

"I'm not digging up. I'm digging down."

"Oh? So the McCloud insolence lives on, does it?"

"Let's hope so."

"And what are you digging down to find if I might ask?"

"I'm digging a grave."

"Oh? A grave is it? And for anybody in particular?"

"For a man who was murdered."

"A mudhole for a man murdered?"

"That's what I said."

"Ah, the McClouds, the McClouds. And who might have murdered the murdered man?"

"No one knows. If they did, wouldn't they have come to you?"

"Who knows what anyone would do? The world, young man, you'll find, is the strangest place in which we're ever going to live. And strangest of all is the people in it. That man there, in the car.

We found him down the road. Imagine biting a gerbil. I don't even want to think about it. Putting it in your mouth—a gerbil—squirming and squealing—how can anyone even think about it—and you bite it! Never would I want to see a thing like that. A gerbil, right there in your mouth. How can anyone even think about it? Imagine!"

"Yes," said Aaron. "I just have. Thank you."

"Squirming———"

"Yes, thank you. And now you must excuse me. I have a murdered man needs burying."

"The insolence of the McClouds thrives and flourishes."

"Thank you. Yes."

Jim finally spoke up. "Pigs need a wallow. You're giving it a good one. I hope it appreciates all you're doing." He turned away then, Tom, too, but only in time to see the prisoner again make his escape. "Now look what you've done!" Jim said. And then, after a series of colorful oaths and a series of grinding turns of the car, they were gone, back in the direction whence they'd come. Aaron, strengthened rather than weakened by the work he'd done, hoisted himself from the grave without difficulty. The elation rightfully known to those who labor was honestly his and, as he went toward the kitchen door, muddied and smelling now of the pig as much as of fish and seaweed and fetid vapors, he couldn't help marveling at the knowledge of this newfound competence as a ditchdigger. Maybe he didn't have to be a writer after all.

When he entered the house, he heard the clink of glasses coming from the living room. He crossed the hall and went inside. There, laid out between two high-backed dining-room chairs was Declan in his coffin, a fine oak box cushioned with a blue quilt with little yellow buttercups and a pillow under his skull, the pillowcase a lighter blue than the quilt, with larger flowers but still buttercups. His Brewers baseball cap had been fitted onto the skull, the peak slanting at an angle over what should have been his face, shading what should have been his eyes and nose. To keep the mouth closed, his thatcher's leggett—an iron tool like a grooved paddle, or an oblong skillet for frying sausages—had been placed in his hands, as if in reverence to his trade, with the paddle part shoved firmly up against his lower jaw. A further act of reverence was a rosary of brown beads entwined in the fingers, binding the two hands together in holy bondage to keep him from committing mischief until hands more blessed than his own might free them into acts of bliss without end.

To complete the shrine Kitty had stuffed a crock with yellow flag and dog violet, with a burst of heather stuck in between to keep the bouquet from seeming too dainty.

Lolly and Kitty were seated on the couch, each holding a glass, Lolly sipping, Kitty staring down, licking her lips, and taking in a deep breath. Sweeney, with a poker, was jabbing among the coals burning in the fireplace.

Aaron had expected a less formal rite: The bones would be placed in the coffin, the coffin would be put in the grave, the mud and earth shoveled on top, and the day's work done. But apparently it was felt that since Sweeney had, with effort and expertise, made the coffin, and Kitty and Lolly had, with quarrel and compromise, placed the bones inside the well-brushed suit, the clean undershorts, the socks, and the clean shirt, their handiwork should not be disposed of too readily.

"We're going to have to use some buckets to get the water out of the hole," Aaron said. "The grave, I mean. Anyone want to help?"

"Sit a minute," said Kitty. "We've all been working away, and it's time for a short rest. Help yourself."

Two more bottles of Tullamore Dew—full liters—had been set on the coffee table. Aaron looked at them, then said, "Maybe I should change."

"For the better?" asked Kitty.

"I'm all wet."

"We're used to that," said Lolly.

"I drink," said Sweeney, "to the man lying there. May God and Mary greet him." He raised his glass in the direction of the coffin, emptied it in a single gulp, and poured himself another glassful. Aaron went to the table, tipped a little whiskey into a glass and made a minimal gesture toward the coffin.

"Is that all you're having?" asked Kitty.

"Maybe after we're finished."

"We *are* finished. All but putting him in the cabbage patch, and that shouldn't take more than a minute."

"Here," said Sweeney. "Make it a good man's portion." He added a few inches to what Aaron had already poured.

"And aren't either of you going to sit down?" Kitty reached over and brushed a book from the easy chair onto the floor. "Kieran Sweeney, to honor the dead—since I know you won't take hospitality from this house and from this family—but to honor the dead as you did just now with a sizable helping of my whiskey, maybe you'll accept a chair in the name of Declan Tovey." She patted the cushion of the easy chair and again brushed the surface even though there was nothing visible that might disturb a man's comfort.

"For Declan Tovey I'll do it." To fortify himself for the treasonous act of sitting down in a McCloud chair in a McCloud house, Sweeney took a goodly gulp, replenished his glass, and sat down on the edge of the cushion Kitty had prepared for him. He'd brought the bottle with him. Was he now, Aaron asked himself, preparing his confession?

For Aaron, if he wanted to sit, there was only the ladder-back chair next to the foot of the coffin. He went over, sat down, and raised his glass, this time in Sweeney's direction, approving of what the man had done—with less difficulty than one might have expected—in sitting where he was sitting.

Water had splashed and soaked itself up into Aaron's khaki shorts and he did his best to sit still so the cloth wouldn't sting and scratch. Behind the coffin the firelight flickered, sending up sudden shafts of light—shadows too—expanding and retracting, the light and dark dancing on the chimney stones as if trying to taunt Declan and mock him for his inability to dance along. Aaron watched, then looked down into his drink. He took another sip and let the whiskey sear down his throat and spread its warmth across his chest. He coughed slightly, then said, "The wind's come up." No one answered, nor was there any need for a reply. The wind itself gave the house a good shake, rattling the shutters and sending a sudden flare of firelight to flicker on the peak of Declan's baseball cap. For extra measure it made the sound of a Halloween ghost along the south side of the house and, to punctuate the cry, slammed a shutter against the kitchen window. Still no one said anything.

Aaron looked at his muddy feet and saw that if he wiggled his toes his toenails would catch some glint of firelight playing under the chairs that supported the coffin. Three times he wiggled them and was about to do it again when Lolly said, "Great were his skills and honest his labor. Any work to be done with his hands would be the work of an artist. Thatching was his trade, but wonders of plumbing were well within his understanding."

Lolly was staring at the chimney wall, catching in her eyes a quick flicker, a light, a shadow. Her glass she had clasped against her right breast, her left hand she held at her throat. "Often didn't we call him in to correct the errors of his licensed inferiors.

The flush toilets of the whole village were given new force at his hands, sufficient in their strength to make sure the contributions would reach the piping that led to the proper station. God greet him." She lifted her glass and took a swig.

"God and Mary too," said Kitty.

Aaron realized it was an Irish wake he was attending, that all the day's preparations led to this event. This is why a coffin was needed and a clothed corpse, this is why the bones were washed and the boards selected from among the finest in the house. This is why the Tullamore Dew had been called into service and why they were all sitting there regarding the oaken box out of which peeped the peak of the cap. Declan Tovey was to be eulogized at last; truths about him would now be told. And, at the end, the confession of the murderer. Lolly had made the introductory speech. Now it was Kitty's turn.

"It was his way with electricity," she said, "that was even more astounding. Never did he make the initial installations—that he left to the licensed. But he had an instinct for appearing a month later, knowing repairs would be needed. The need, of course, was not obvious to all. Only Declan could detect it and do the work that brought correction. Few words if any were ever spoken, but we had to give only a few nods of middling understanding and the man would go about his work. What patience, and so solemn too. And when he'd finished, he'd simply call out he'd collect his wage the next time through. And lo and behold, gladly was he paid when the time came round. To no one's wonderment, the electric bills had seen a sudden dip and the extortionate rates brought into line with what a family could afford to pay. How this had been achieved no one knew, and no one asked to know. And when the utility did its investigation as to why certain areas were less needful of their electricity, no discoveries were made. Concluded it was that we backward souls lived mostly in darkness and refused to be civilized by the use of appliances no respectable household would be without. And it was Declan did it. And God and Mary save him."

"And Brendan and Patrick besides," added Sweeney—whose turn it was now to speak.

Aaron took another sip and then a decent gulp. The whiskey warmed him and gave him some small comfort in his wet clothes and cold feet.

"And let it not be forgotten," Sweeney intoned, "that he performed common tasks with uncommon skill. Gutters he could clean and drains he could scrape and any repair you could name would be done before the day itself was done. He could build a chimney that would keep the warm in and the smoke out and put back in business a dry stone wall that could pass for part of an ancient oratory or a chapel for Christian worship. And let the devil take him for all of that."

"For all of that," said Lolly.

"For all of that," said Kitty.

Sweeney poured more Dew into his own glass, then into Kitty's, then into Lolly's. He put the bottle back, then noticed Aaron. He brought the bottle over, all but filled the glass to the brim, then, after a quick glance into the coffin, went back and sat down, this time moving a little farther back on the cushion. He sat erect, looking down into his whiskey, then drew himself up ever more erect. He's going to confess, Aaron thought. The precise moment had come. Of course it was Sweeney. He was jealous of something real or imagined between Declan Tovey and his aunt. Sweeney killed the man. And now it would all come out. Savoring the moment, Aaron swirled the whiskey in his glass, spilling some, but creating a small vortex on the surface. He would drink to Sweeney's health after he'd made his confession.

But it was Lolly who spoke. "Great as was his work, some suspicion was always in attendance. He would appear and disappear, an itinerant if not a born Traveler, a Tinker. He had no known wife to give him respectability, no known children to impose respect for the common codes. He spoke little, an indication in itself that all was not right with him. God gave us speech so we could speak. He had no wit that anyone had ever heard, another proof that he was of a species foreign to these parts. That he never danced or sang could be excused: God gives his gifts at his whim and withholds them at his pleasure. If it pleased God that the feet of Declan Tovey be ignorant of rhythm and that his throat be the envy of a crow, that's God's own business and holy is his name. But worse still, he was never heard to laugh, not by anyone who had ever come forward to give testimony. And these are things that must be said."

Sweeney poured more whiskey, emptying the bottle into his glass, then going for a fresh bottle on the far end of the table. Kitty, meanwhile, had taken up this second phase of the wake where less than flattering subjects were mentioned after the eulogies had been gotten safely out of the way. "Laugh, maybe not. But he could smile. And did. And to that there's been more testimony than the towns around can bear to hear. It wasn't a smile that reached for the ears, just a little lifting at the two corners, with the lips parting to show two rows of gleaming teeth obviously crafted by the devil himself. And at this showing something would happen to the eyes. They would send forth light from a world within, a world of wonders and of puzzling promises. A temptation and a dare, the eyes—they invited one and all to attempt the journey that might take them to the hidden land. No charts were given, no compass offered to point the way. There was only the wonder and the promise and the dare and the light. And what I've said is true, so help me heaven."

This, thought Aaron, was preamble to confession if ever he'd heard one. She'd loved him, pursued him, lost him, and killed him. Wasn't he taken up from her own garden? From under her own cabbages? This was difficult to believe of one's own kin, and Aaron considered speaking up himself, to tell her to go no further. To keep her trap shut for a change. There was no need for more words to be said out loud.

Sweeney, as if to reward her for her speech, was providing her with more Dew. Aaron must say something before it would be too late.

But the next words came not from Kitty but from Sweeney. "Pilgrims searching for the hidden land," he said, "and there were more than many—ardent in their efforts, desperate in their supplications, mindless in their offerings, but no one is known to have reached the light lurking behind the eyes of Declan Tovey. No one had made the quest and returned with some trophy proving a destination reached. The roadsides have been strewn with fallen pilgrims, with those supplicants who could go no further and begged only that the light might shine but one more time. And Declan might smile his smile at such a foolish thought, only to give increase to the anguish already felt. His own eyes were blind. None of the wreckage did he see. But that he should, for the common good, be done away with was evident to many. Or at least to me."

Now it was Aaron who got up and filled the glasses all around. A drink should be at the ready for what Sweeney was about to say. He would now confess. But this, too, Aaron did not want to hear. Sweeney was a good and honorable man. He'd saved Aaron's life. He should, with heaven's intervention, be given to Kitty and Kitty to him. He mustn't speak. But it was too late. Sweeney's mouth was opening.

"I," said Sweeney, rising to his feet, "I am now going to sing a

song." And he did, the melody sprightly, the rhythm a happy lilt
that invited the beat of a drum or the clap of the hands.

> 'Tis the best of the doctor's prescriptions
> If whiskey and porter are cheap,
> For it cures us of all our afflictions
> And puts all men's sorrows to sleep.
> And the old woman, wheezing and groaning,
> A-bed for a year in despair,
> When she sups her half pint, stops her moaning,
> And kicks the bedclothes in the air."

Kitty gave an uncharacteristic squeal of delight, and Lolly guf-
fawed outright. Sweeney obliged with a reprise, his voice, to Aaron's
surprise, not a fine Irish tenor as would seem fit for a wake, but a
good growl of a basso, created to proclaim profundities not quite
similar to the one he was expounding now. Before he had finished—

> 'Tis the best of the doctor's prescriptions
> If whiskey and porter are cheap,
> For it cures us of all our afflictions
> And puts all men's sorrows to sleep.

Kitty got up and, with an approving shriek, began to dance,
her arms at her sides, but her legs and feet performing a complexity of movements that easily compensated for—and defeated—
any inhibition the rest of the body might try to enforce. Out
would go a leg, the feet then driven by this display to an even further frenzy, disciplined but defiant. When the leg shot out a second time, Lolly had no choice but to clap her hands to the beat of
the song, then stand up herself and make her own contibution to

the sacrilege. Shouts and squeals helped drive them both—Lolly and Kitty—to an even higher pitch of unauthorized abandon. Twice, three times, the coffin was kicked, the peak of Declan's cap shifting from side to side to acknowledge the blows. The firelight flared higher, offering its own giddy tribute to the occasion, the flickering lights and shadows tickling and taunting the corpse, a sudden glare catching one of the rosary beads, a lengthening flame stroking the left cheekbone, a shadow nudging a shoulder, the flames themselves an unfeeling temptress sent to mock the un-fleshed bones of the helpless dead.

Into the third reprise Sweeney too took up the dance, clumsy at first, then tapping and stomping and kicking with all the sure-ness that only a great joy could inspire. The movements of his feet failed to diminish the strength of his voice. It was as if the motion of his legs, like bellows, pumped added air into his lungs, giving an even greater sonority and force to the song.

"But—but you loved this man, this man lying here," Aaron said. No one heard him. With the dancing, the shouts and squeals rose to near dementia. Again the coffin was kicked. Again Declan rocked a bit and then was still. Even the house seemed to shudder and shake beneath their feet, and the wind outside raised a howl of its own to drive them on to a more complete possession of de-monic proportions.

The screams and shrieks, and the wind, too, rose to a new pitch. Then there was a tearing sound, and another shudder shook the house. Additional feet had taken up the dance but in a rhythm of their own. The pig had come clattering into the room. It had torn through the screen door. Its hooves tippity-tapped on the wooden floor, its snout raised, its squeals and screeches a worthy reinforcement of the general madness.

Louder still sang Sweeney:

And the old woman, wheezing and groaning,
A-bed for a year in despair,
When she sups her half pint, stops her moaning,
And kicks the bedclothes in the air.

Faster danced Lolly and Kitty. The pig raced around the couch, knocking over an end table, around an easy chair, trampled on some books, around the coffee table, screaming, threatening the Tullamore Dew. On the dancing went and the song too. More kicks were given the coffin, and the laughter came close to a cry of pain, the song a protest shouted into the demented noise. The pig was headed for the coffin.

Aaron jumped up. "It's going to tip him over!" He called out the words, but even they were taken as a goad to further excitement. The pig lowered its head and aimed itself directly at the coffin. Aaron sprang into its path and spread wide his arms. The pig continued its charge, butting its way through the pandemonium. When it was within two feet of the coffin, Aaron, as if joining the festivities at last, flung out his leg and gave the pig a swift shove on its left ham. The pig, stunned, stopped and looked with disbelief at Aaron. Aaron gave it another shove, harder. The pig spent one full moment in stupefied amazement, then let out a scream never heard this side of the slaughterhouse.

"You can't do this to the poor man. He's dead," Aaron cried out to the pig, a plea for acknowledgment if not understanding. He gave the pig another shove.

Lolly stopped first, then Sweeney—and the song stopped too. Kitty slowed down, then she too was still. They all—the pig included—stared at Aaron.

Lolly reared back a little. "You kicked the pig," she said, her voice astonished and threatening in equal measure.

"It was going to tip over—to spill out——"

Kitty took a step forward. "You kicked the pig?"

Sweeney looked from Aaron to Lolly to Kitty. "He kicked the pig?"

"He kicked it," Lolly said.

Sweeney looked again at Aaron. "Did you kick the pig?" he asked.

Aaron gave the pig another push. "Yes," he said. "I kicked the pig."

Again the pig protested.

"But why?"

"It was going to tip over the coffin. To spill out all the bones."

In unison all three looked at the coffin. They then looked at Aaron himself, their heads moving at the same pace, each expression equally bewildered by the strangeness of his concern and the enormity of his deed.

Kitty moved to the coffin, reached inside, and touched the tips of her fingers to the side of the skull. Without taking her hand away, she said, "Let the sweet bones rest. I was the one killed him with the hand that's touching him now."

No one moved except the pig. It was trying to root into the rug near the couch, scratching its snout, snorting into the weave. "The things he said to me should never have been said," Kitty continued. "The only time—or so he told me—the only time he'd ever laughed in all his life was when he read one of my books. It was the one amusement he'd ever found in the whole sorrowing world. My correction of *Jane Eyre* sent him, he claimed, howling to the skies. And he dared to open a book lying there on the kitchen table, where, in my correction of *Jude the Obscure*, all the children grow up and go to Cambridge. He read from it. And he laughed. He read some more. And laughed again. Mid-sentence I gave him the clout with the implement you see in his hands now, dispatching him to the devil that had created him in his very own image. And I buried him where he would feed my cabbages."

"No!" said Aaron. "That's not true. I know it isn't. Sweeney, sing your song. I shouldn't have kicked the pig. Please. Sing!"

Without taking her hand from Declan's cheekbone, Kitty said, "It's the truth I've told, and there's no one stopping me now."

"Kieran Sweeney," Aaron pleaded, "for the love of God, sing! Don't let her——" Sweeney reached out his hand and placed it on the crown of the baseball cap. "No need for me to sing, nor need for you to worry. There's no word of truth in what's been said. Never did this woman kill this man, and I'm the only one can know for sure. It was by the hand that touches him now that he died, and justly so, whatever the law might say. Standing straight before me in the mist of a misty day, he said words no man may dare to say. The woman in question, the one he referred to, has not, as he claimed, the face of a cow. In her all beauty of the world lives in shining splendor, cowface or no cowface. And when he threw in for bad measure that the woman in question—the one I love and will love for all my days and all my nights and well into eternity until God commands me to look his beatific way instead—he said that this lump of a woman had twice farted in his presence and had the hair of a hag. It was then that justice was done, not with a sword but with the iron he grips in his fist right now. 'Cowface,' said I. 'Fart!' said I. 'Hag!' said I, giving a blow each time. And he was done for. And I buried him in the garden then of the woman herself and let him try as he might to see her cowface now."

Kitty turned a stony gaze in Sweeney's direction, but before she could say anything, Lolly stood upright, came closer to the coffin and chose, for the placement of her hand, the leggett itself. "Be that as it may, Kieran Sweeney, no one here has said what's true in all this time, and so I'll say it now. The blow was struck by

me, and it didn't take more than one, as it took some others I'll
never name. True, a man should be careful what he says about another's loved one, and my deed is the proof of that. Scorn my pigs,
he did, and lie his lies. Stupid, he called them. Filthy, he said. Ate
swill and shit and slurry, he said. Not my pigs, I said, a warning
already in my eye. But would he stop? No. Not Declan Tovey. He
must point to a pig just four feet off and call out within the pig's
hearing, 'Stupid! Filthy! Eat swill and shit and slurry. You,' he
cried, 'You're the one I'm talking about.' And then he did it, seal-
ing his doom. Over he strode, the four feet of it and—and I don't
want to say it. But he did it and it has to be told. He kicked the
pig."

Aaron stood up straighter, then slumped as low as he could
and still remain standing. The pig raised its snout from the rug.

"One sharp blow and the devil was down, and the leg that had
desecrated the pig stretched out straight as a candle. And because
I'd seen the cabbages planted that day, I knew the fitting place to
put him, and it's God's own justice that a pig brought him to the
light so we can put him back into the cabbages where he belongs."

She kicked the coffin.

"No!" said Aaron. "You're all lying. You're—you're—you're
competing. You're all claiming credit—or—or protecting each
other or—or you're *competing*. You each want to be the most important person in his life! I don't want to hear any of this. I didn't
hear any of this. Sweeney, sing again. Sing and we'll dance, all of
us. I'll dance. I promise. Sing. Please."

When no voice was raised, Aaron himself began to sing,
weakly but with some brave determination.

> We let the pigs in the parlor,
> We let the pigs in the parlor,
> We let the pigs . . .

His voice grew in strength and conviction.

> . . . in the parlor,
> We let the pigs in the parlor,
> And they are Irish, too.

The wind gave the house another shake, shuddering the frame, causing even the stones to groan. Lolly was looking at Aaron now, not with scorn or threat but with a mournful disappointment, questioning why he had done what he had done.

He continued to sing, his voice a reedy tenor that made up in volume and vigor what it lacked in timbre, its pitch uncertain, its passion beyond doubt. He looked directly at Lolly.

> We let the pigs in the parlor,
> We let the pigs in the parlor,
> We let the pigs in the——

A cry of heartrending anguish was heard above the singing, followed by a series of shrieks obviously prompted by a pain beyond what could be endured. The pig, to escape from the song, ran clattering from the room, across the hall, through the kitchen, and out the hole it had torn in the screen door. The shrieks, instead of receding, became louder until, finally, a great splash was heard and the sounds were reduced to snorts, an expression of revulsion and disgust.

"It's in the grave—again!" Sweeney bolted out of the room, fast in the path of the pig. The screen door slammed. "It's in the grave!" he shouted from the yard. Kitty followed, and again the screen door slammed. Lolly apparently had hoped to make it through the door before it closed but failed by a hair. Aaron, still singing, heard an *"Ahgh"* followed by the opening, then slam-ming, of the door.

The song trailed off. He sat down on the ladder-back chair, the only mourner left. The fire in the fireplace was dying down, sending out onto the chimney stones only a muted glow that wouldn't last much longer. Outside the wind had found the note it had been searching for, high and shrill, neither rising nor falling, but insistent and alarmed. It rattled the windows, it ha-rassed the chimney, and, it seemed to Aaron, nudged the whole house to remind it that the elements were taking its measure. Now the note lowered itself an entire octave. Aaron listened to its call, a summons to whatever furies might be passing through, an invitation to join it in the terror it was determined to bestow.

Above and through it all came the cries from the garden, pleas and threats to the pig, blandishments and calls of *"Suueee! Suueee!"* a splash, a screech, a shriek, Lolly's voice the loudest of all. Aaron looked through the screen door and saw, by the light of a gibbous moon, the three figures dancing around the grave, bending down to it, raising their arms to heaven, circling the pig as if it were an object of worship, continuing the rites and revels that had earlier consecrated the coffin.

Aaron couldn't move except for an occasional blink and the rise and fall of his breath. Lolly McKeever had broken his heart. The mournful gaze she'd turned on him, the bewildered hurt he'd seen in her face, in her eyes, and in the helpless lowering of her chin, had not only loosened his heart but had, as well, wounded it and made it susceptible to invasion.

Phila Rambeaux had played out the part the Fates had, from the start, devised. She had sent Aaron to these shores, dispatched him toward his truer destiny, and could now fade from the scene with less than a smattering of applause. It was to Lolly he had been sent. All events, all persons, had no purpose but to bring him to this moment.

The wind in its ravings shouldered the house, as if trying to uproot it and send it off to Cork, shoving rather then blasting it, nudging, pushing. Aaron wished it would take the roof and be satisfied. In the yard the pleas and calls had taken the form of laughter, high and howling; there was another splash, a yell, and Aaron could see Kitty and Lolly lifting Sweeney by his arms, up out of the grave.

The room shuddered, the glasses rattling on the tabletop, a chattering comment on what was taking place. Aaron headed for the glass he'd left half empty on the coffee table but stumbled against the edge of the coffin. He drew himself up and looked at the unfleshed face of the murdered Declan, the murder weapon held fast in his hands.

> The grave's a fine and private place,
> But none I think do there embrace.

Aaron lurched toward the table, took up his glass, and gulped down all that was left. The house shuddered again, more deeply than before. He put the glass down and picked up what Kitty had left. That, too, he took in one good swig. Again the house shuddered, which he took as an incitement to help himself to Sweeney's glass. That too he drank. When he'd lifted Lolly's glass, fuller than the others, he turned toward Declan and raised the glass in sad salute, but before he could bring it to his lips, the floor trembled beneath him, rattling the coffin and toppling the ladder-back chair. He steadied himself with one hand on the coffin's edge, then made another attempt to drain the drink. But again there was the shudder, a lamp crashing. The foot end of the coffin bounced from its chair; the windows rattled frantically. A rumble came next, then a low roar, growing, beneath the house. The light went out. Only the silver glow of the moon lit the room. The coals of the fire were hurled across the floor, a pile of embers lodged beneath the tipped end of the coffin.

Still clinging to Lolly's glass, Aaron started toward the door, the hall, the kitchen, the yard outside. But before he could make it out of the room, only halfway to the door, he felt the floor lowering slowly, like an unhurried elevator. He made another effort toward the door, but a slight tilt made it an uphill struggle. The roar was even louder now, the war cry of a beast about to set upon its prey.

The house began to wobble. Flames were lapping at the tumbled end of the coffin, wisps of smoke were rising from the rug. Aaron called out for help using the one word he could still speak: "Lolly!"

Such was the tilt of the floor that he could no longer see into the yard itself, but only the trees on the far side of the garden. "Lolly!" he called again, the cry devoured by the animal roar coming from underneath the house. He got the glass to his lips, gulped the Dew, and swallowed fast. The glass fell from his hand, the floor pitched sideways, and he was thrown against the coffin flaming at its foot.

Aaron dropped to all fours and began his angled climb to where he knew the door to be. He was in the hall. He was in the kitchen, the hole in the screen just ahead.

Water touched his foot, then slowly rose to cover his leg to the knee. The sea was coming in, rising behind him in the tilted house. The house was being pulled down into the sea itself, giving the adamant waves the prize they'd been seeking for uncounted years. The wind, with its pushes and shoves, had done its best to send the house to safer ground, but the sea had proved more powerful.

Aaron had been warned. The sea had asked for him by name, had staked its claim, and now had come to take the chosen trophy, which had twice escaped its unfathomable embrace. .

The roaring stopped, distant rumblings and tumblings were heard, a sudden crash of stone on stone, and the water rushed through the screen door. Aaron sprang toward the opening and scraped through just as the water rose to the top of the tear the pig had made. Except it was not the water rising; it was the house descending, sinking, the waves washing through it, over it, welcoming it to its final rest.

Aaron began his upward swim, struggling to the top. He reached the air. A wave, by way of recognition, crested over his head. Again he struggled, again he made it to the air. Before the next wave pounded him down, he saw the shore ahead, the tumbled rocks, great slabs of stone, the torn cliff and the newly created cove where the house had stood. He saw three figures at the cliff's edge, silhouetted against the moon, waving.

Determined not to panic, Aaron stroked the water, pulling himself toward land, but the waves were not willing to surrender so easily, so quickly, the mere mortal who seemed reluctant to accept their favors. One after another they fell on him, less angry now, more conciliatory, as if making a case for their benevolence. Aaron would have none of it. On and on he struggled.

It was the shore, not the sea, that now betrayed him. It kept receding, withdrawing from him, unwilling to accept him whom the sea, with such effort, had come to claim. The cliffs had been brutalized enough. Further resistance would bring only further wounding. Already the rock face had been sheared away, stone torn from stone and thrown one upon another, broken and shattered and soon to be milled to sand. The time for peace had come, a truce declared, the sought-after soul delivered to the fate decreed by the sea itself and obviously endorsed by the gods. It was useless

for Aaron to fight, abandoned as he was by the land that had nur-
tured and sustained him for all his life.

To announce the end, a fish began to nose his thigh, bumping
itself against his leg. He would resist, then surrender. Again the
fish, huge, poked at him. Aaron thrashed the water with his leg.
The fish seemed to withdraw, but probably only to ready itself for
the next assault, which would, he was sure, be the final one. Then
he felt the fish slide along his side, slipping ahead of him through
the water. Now it was bobbing in front of him. His outstretched
hand, close to its last failing stroke, hit against it. It was not a fish.
There, before his eyes, was the canoe, its previous occupant
nowhere to be seen. The canoe rose to the crest of a wave, with
Aaron rising too. Now the canoe descended, and Aaron as well.
Exhausted, he managed to climb inside. There was no paddle. He
lay down in the bow, barely able to breathe, his feet lifted onto the
seat. There he lay, the waves under him sending him high, lowering him down only to raise him up again. Perhaps he had drowned
and this was the vaunted peace promised to those who surrender
at last. But overhead was the moon. Under him was the discomfort of the wooden slats ribbing the canoe. There were his feet,
cleansed of the mud brought up out of the grave. Aaron lifted his
head, then shifted around to face the shore. It was no longer receding. It was coming nearer, drawing him to itself, all discord at an
end, all treacheries reversed. And there, on the edge of the torn
cliff, three figures danced.

Closer and closer came the shore. Steadily the canoe rode the
waves. Aaron sat upright, waiting to be delivered. Now the three
figures were running, sliding, falling, grabbing onto one another,
running again down the narrow switchback steps leading to the
shore. Shouts, screams, loud and raucous cries—all were caught in
the wind and hurled into the tumult of the upper air. A few feet
from shore, the wave, by way of a farewell, made a great heave,

crashing down on top of him, then flinging his body, heart, mind, and soul out onto the rock-strewn beach, a "good riddance to bad rubbish" if ever there was one.

Now he could hear the shouts coming closer. Words reached his ears. "God and Mary and all the angels." It was Kitty. Then "And Patrick and Brendan too." That would be Kieran Sweeney. And then, closer still, Lolly's piteous "And all the saints besides."

Aaron was almost on his feet when the three flung themselves on him, sending all four into a heap, Aaron on the bottom, half in, half out of the canoe. With repeated prayers and screaming cries, they untangled themselves and managed to haul Aaron further onto the beach and prop him upright. With heaving breath, he tried to speak, but again, as before, the sea had taken from him the gift of speech and had given him instead a mouth that could only wobble open, then shut, then open again.

To celebrate and confirm his survival, Kitty, then Lolly and Sweeney, began to brush him off as if he had risen from the dust and not from the sea. Twice under their ministrations he almost fell but was duly yanked up. As if they had finally managed, with their pattings and brushings, to make him presentable, they stepped away to view their handiwork. Aaron tried to speak but still to no effect, possibly because he had not the least idea what it was he wanted to say.

Lolly, looking at him with a sly and insolent smile, gave him his cue. "Now that you're saved and all, can you, do you think, can you love someone might be a murderer?"

Aaron's mouth ceased its wobble, locked as it was in an open position. He could not move, not even to shiver or to blink or to twitch. It was Sweeney who spoke first, taking into his hand the hand of Kitty. "I can," he said. "I can love someone might be a murderer."

Kitty, aghast at first at the touch of a Sweeney hand, soon nodded her head in resignation. "I can," she said, "murderer as you well
may be." She turned to Aaron. "And Aaron, you? After all, isn't it
a chance everyone has to take if ever we're going to love at all?"

Aaron turned to Lolly and blurted out the words given to him
at last. "I can! I can! I swear I can!"

At the top of the cliff the joined lovers paused to gaze silently out
over the sea still booming and plunging beneath them, the gibbous moon making its destined descent into the far side of the
horizon. It was Sweeney who spoke. "It's a great grave you've been
given, Declan Tovey, greater by far than the mudhole we were arranging ourselves. Lie now in peace. Your mystery may not be
solved, but it is accepted in all its unfathomable glory as God
prompts us to do, and we will live with it for the rest of all our
days. And for pity's sake, don't go sending your old bones back up
floating onto the shore and raising ructions all over again. You've
done the deeds you were meant to do. All is fulfilled."

The wind howled, the sea raged. And the pig came to stand
beside them, motionless, snout upraised, meditating perhaps on
what had come to pass and contemplating as well what was still to
come.

ACKNOWLEDGMENTS

The author offers unending thanks to Yaddo, in Saratoga Springs, New York, and to the Cill Rialaig Project, in County Kerry, Ireland. He is also grateful to the Irish writer Eamon Sweeney for his help and encouragement and to Tara Claire O'Donoghue, Catherine Clarke, Daniel D'Arezzo, Don Ettlinger, Rebecca Stowe, David Barbour, Bruce Hunter, Martha Witt, Linda Porter—with a special expression of gratitude to Robert Cohan for his help and instructions in Irish darts—how to win, how to lose. To my nephew Jim Smith, my thanks for the accomplished transfer of my sloppy typescript to an acceptable computer printout, and to my brother-in-law Tom Smith, for copyediting said printout—arduous and not particularly thrilling tasks, done with good cheer and uncommon expertise.

A special thanks beyond the power of words to my tenacious agent, Wendy Weil, and her associate, Emily Forland, for their empathic help and unfailing encouragements.

Also to Barbara Lazear Ascher, the editor whose enthusiasm made possible this publication.

The first chapter from

The Pig Comes to Dinner

sequel to *The Pig Did It*

Kitty McCloud, hack novelist of global repute, paced the pebbled courtyard of her recently acquired home—one Castle Kissane—on the pretext that she was waiting for her newly acquired husband, Kieran Sweeney, to arrive with his truckload of cows, thereby completing the domestic arrangements that would prove their conjugal claim to be, in the truest sense, a household in the age-old tradition of County Kerry, Ireland.

Although she had not articulated to herself the real reason for the repeated frantic backing and forthing—first in the direction of Crohan Mountain, which bordered their property in the northwest, then to the castle road on the south—she was, in reality, tormenting her imagination, determined to summon from its fertile depths a possible "correction" she planned to write to George Eliot's big mess of a novel, *The Bloody Mill on the Bloody Floss*—the added expletives a measure of Kitty's consternation. The continuation of her career depended on her highly successful ability to pillage novels from the commonly accepted canon and rescue them from the misguided efforts of their celebrated authors.

What she hoped for was a rare insight similar to the one

she had applied to Charlotte Brontë's *Jane Eyre*—in which it is Rochester who throws himself from the attic in despair over Jane's rejection of a bigamous marriage, after which Jane, with her goodness and kindness, tames the Madwoman, and the two of them create for themselves a life of calm contentment fulfilled by weaving, making pottery, and the practice of animal husbandry.

So far, none of the possibilities for *The Mill* provoked her imagination into the state of high excitement and imperative promise without which she could do nothing. For her, only a near-hysterical propulsion would allow her to proceed, and she was, at the moment, grounded in an inertia that refused her every attempt to create even the slightest stir, let alone the volcanic eruption she so desperately craved.

Whether she should curse Ms. Eliot or her heroine, Maggie Tulliver, for this intransigence was not yet decided. (Never did Ms. McCloud consider that the source of the difficulty might lie within herself. Such a consideration lay well beyond even *her* considerable powers.) She raised her gaze to the top of the mounded hill that was Crohan Mountain and saw nothing but heather and gorse and a scattering of oblong stones, whitened with age. She turned to the castle road, praying that the truck would soon arrive and provide some surcease from her torment.

To some degree, her prayer was answered. Indeed, a truck was approaching. But instead of the arrival of the expected cows, as so often happens with prayers the answer came in a form much less welcome. There, moving toward her, *was* a small truck—what in America would be called a pickup—but it was one identifiable as belonging to her American nephew, Aaron McCloud, and his recent bride, Lolly McKeever, now

also a McCloud. In itself, their approach could not be considered a cause for concern. They might be coming to help welcome the cows or to invite themselves to supper, or to
commit some lesser intrusion.

What roused in Kitty no small suspicion that something
more complicated might be involved was the presence, in the
bed of the truck, of a pig. A pig all too familiar and not at all
welcome. Its snout was raised to take in the castle air, its
cloven hooves apparently firmly planted in the bed of the
truck to counter the bounce and rattle over the uneven road.

For the first time since Kitty had bought Castle Kissane,
she wished it didn't lack the full complement of a moat and
the attendant drawbridge, to say nothing of a portcullis that
could be lowered in situations such as the arrival of this particular pig. The castle, to be sure, was not without its charms.
It could claim a courtyard in which dogs might take the afternoon sun (should there be a sun). There were stables and
sheds in arcades from which the healthy stench of manure
could find its way into the great hall, where matters of state
and strategies of defense had once been argued into incomprehension. At the top of its turret, reachable by a winding
stone staircase at the end of a passageway that led past the
conjugal bedroom, one could pace in the open air and participate in the life of the Kerry countryside. One could see the
snow-dusted summits of Macgillicuddy's Reeks; one could
count cows and sheep and search the horizon of the Western
Sea for ships of friendly or unfriendly intent. One could smell
the salt air, even at this distance, or the fragrant scent of gorse
and heather, hawthorn and honeysuckle.

But truth to be told, the castle wasn't all that much. With
its two-story crude stone bulk and its four-story turret, it

resembled nothing so much as the architectural progenitor of a design that would find its ultimate statement on the central plains of America: the barn and silo—except that this mighty archetype was built for the ages. And, most to be regretted at the moment, it contained no keep into which Kitty could now withdraw, as had the populous of old, to escape unwanted encroachments.

Now, in the bed of the approaching truck, an unwanted intrusion was looking for all the world as if it had just won first prize at the fair and was being given a royal progress throughout the county, accepting with easy indifference the obeisance of those privileged enough to line its path.

So that it wouldn't seem that Kitty had been simply standing there as if waiting to welcome an unwelcome pig, and to let her nephew and his bride know that they were interrupting her at a task of some import, she gave a quick wave and, as best she could, tried to make it appear that she had been, before their arrival, on the way to the farthest of the courtyard sheds. There, in a great heap, was the refuse left behind by the previous tenants of the castle, who happened to be squatters: the stained mattresses, the broken lamps, the computer parts either obsolete or damaged in moments of exasperation; a broken guitar; shoes, boots, and sandals, most without mates; college texts (one in economics), tattered paperbacks (two of them Kitty's inimitable triumphs), magazines, and more than several works written in Irish, not only Peig Sayers, the bane of everyone's schooling, whose Irish writings were force-fed down their gagging throats, but also Sean O'Conaill and Tomás Ó' Criomhthain; and, crowning the pile, a television set with what appeared to be a kicked-in screen.

When the truck pulled to a stop, Kitty's nephew, Aaron, got out of its cab. He was wearing khaki pants, a red sweatshirt emblazoned with the word WISCONSIN, and a pair of muddy sneakers. Lolly dismounted from the passenger side. She was wearing a pair of oversized woolen pants, so large indeed that they could easily have belonged to some former lover who had left them behind on one of his more than several visits to the all-too-accommodating Lolly in the days—and nights—gone by.

Not infrequently did Lolly affect this attire. At times, Kitty considered it a permissibly mocking statement relative to her chosen profession of swineherd. A womanly pig person could surely be allowed to doff her fitted jeans and designer boots and don the obvious castoffs more appropriate to the disgusting chores her calling required.

In less charitable moments—of which there were a considerable number—Kitty convinced herself that Lolly McKeever, now Lolly McCloud, was indeed flaunting, for all to see, some past lover. That she could continue to indulge in this unseemly display even after her marriage to Kitty's nephew was surely an invitation to outrage. But Kitty counseled herself to refrain from a direct challenge during which she would have hurled not accusations but known truths that would shame even Lolly, who was, in most circumstances, almost as impervious as Kitty herself to any assault on her self-assured perfections.

Let her nephew—who, by the idiosyncrasies of Irish procreation, was only two years younger than herself—discover for himself, in the context of his precipitous marriage, the true nature of the hussy he had so ignorantly wed. Kitty would neither do nor say anything that might disturb the pre-

sumed bliss her nephew and her best friend Lolly—the slut—
were inflicting on each other.

That Aaron, himself a writer, had failed to see more accurately the truth about his bride, that his perceptions were so
faulty, Kitty accepted as the reason he was of a renown so distant from her own. Had he possessed his aunt's incomparable
discernments, surely he, too, could have carried his bride
across a castle threshold instead of installing himself in his
wife's house, well within calling distance of the sty that gave
their home its defining distinction. Because competition was
never a consideration, Kitty felt quite free to praise and
encourage him in the exercise of his decidedly inferior gifts.

As Kitty emerged from these reflections, Aaron went to
the truck's tailgate, lowered it, and encouraged the pig to
jump down, which it did with improbable ease. Without so
much as a snort of greeting, it bounded down the slope
toward the stream that flowed along the foot of Crohan
Mountain. As she watched it cavort, Kitty experienced a
growing certainty that some unilateral decision regarding the
pig had already taken place.

Aaron and Lolly now stood before Kitty, smiling, signaling
that Kitty's good nature was about to be taxed.

"We brought you the pig," Lolly said.

"Really?" said Kitty.

"We thought it would be better off here," Aaron added.

"How considerate." Kitty, too, smiled.

At that moment, like a cavalry reinforcement coming to
the rescue at the most needed time, there came around the
turn onto the castle road Kieran and the cows.

The truck pulled up at the far side of the courtyard. Kieran jumped out, slammed the cab door, nodded to Lolly and to Aaron, went to his wife, took her into his arms, and put his mouth against hers—crunching his tawny, well-trimmed beard against her tender cheek, keeping open his blazing blue eyes even when they could see no more than the right side of Kitty's forehead, a strand of sweet black hair, and the upper curve of her lovely ear.

Kieran removed his lips, let his beard spring back into place, and reclaimed his arms, all the while, with still blazing eyes, piercing Kitty to the pit of her stomach with the now familiar warning that she prepare herself for further stirrings yet to come. Kitty, in good wifely fashion, seared his eyes with hers, neither of them blinking—a metaphor, perhaps, for the marriage recently contracted. Kieran turned and strode back toward the truck.

Lolly called to Kieran, "You want some help with the cows?"

"I think I can manage, but thanks."

With an overly casual walk indicating she was trying to make an unnoted departure, Lolly moved toward her own truck. "Maybe we should just go, then," she said airily.

With an overstated indifference all her own, Kitty, not without an undercurrent of resolve, said, "I think you might want first to go fetch your pig."

Kieran caught the word. He paused in his efforts to move the cows. "Pig? What pig?"

"Kieran, sweetheart," said Kitty, "there's only one pig. And it's here."

"What's it doing here?"

"That has yet to be explained."

"First, let me get the herd down to the mire."

The cows, huddled together, seemed reluctant to accept the invitation to go wallow in the bog. Some raised their massive heads and bellowed, convinced that it was to the slaughter they'd been brought and not to the greener ground awaiting at the bottom of the ramp.

Kieran, with the agility of a goat, jumped aboard and, with a nudge here and a slap there, began more of a shifting than a movement toward the incline. The cows stepped daintily, their hooves touching lightly on the weathered planks, proving to one and all that they were ladies of considerable refinement, their swaying udders and a single deposit of cow flop notwithstanding.

Now that the work was mostly done, Sly, Kieran's border collie, entrusted with disciplining the cows, bounded down the hill, having already left territorial claims at the sheds, the foundation stones of the castle, and the rock wall that hedged the apple orchard west of the roadway. Tail wagging, it happily moved among the cows, nipping shanks, barking, and generally making sure that the time for serenity had come to an end.

The pig returned from the stream and presented itself to its old acquaintance, Kieran Sweeney, snout raised as if it detected on the man's person some hidden delectable that would now be surrendered.

"*Faugh a Ballagh!*" "Get out of the way!" Kieran, who was returning to the truck to shovel out manure left behind by an indifferent cow, bent down and clapped his hands close to the pig's ears and repeated the words any Irish pig should understand, "*Faugh a Ballagh!*" He then jumped up onto the truck, shovel in hand.

The pig trotted into the castle courtyard, stopping midway to lower its head and slowly move its snout over the pebbles like a mine detector searching out buried objects. That it refrained from rooting and turning the entire courtyard upside down allowed Kitty to return her attention to Lolly and her nephew. "Should we assume," she said, "that your place has been destroyed by our friend here and now it's our turn?"

Lolly jerked her head back, aghast. "Not at all!"

"It's become quite docile." Aaron weakened his smile to indicate that he was lying.

"It's our present to you. The two of you," Lolly said, expressing a newly arrived thought. "A gift. Since you'll be doing some farming now, surely you should have yourselves a pig."

"All right, then," said Kitty. "Now tell me what's wrong. Why the pig? Why here? Why us?"

"Well . . ." said Lolly.

"Yes. Go on."

"Well . . ." Lolly turned toward her husband and whispered, "You tell her."

"No, it's all right. You're doing fine."

"All right, then." Lolly looked directly at Kitty, raising her head so that her chin and her nose made a show of being loftily indifferent to how her words were to be received. "We can't have it in the herd." She took in a quick breath to strengthen her resolve. "It's a lesbian."

"A lesbian?"

Lolly took in a longer breath. "It—it keeps—well—performing 'proprietary acts' on the females."

Before Kitty could respond, Aaron spoke up. "The females don't seem to mind, but the males, they—well—they get a bit exercised."

"Men!" said Kitty, snorting.

"Then you'll keep it?" Lolly's eyes widened in hope, then deepened into pleading. "I can't find it in my heart to sell it or, well, you know."

"Slaughter it? Is that what you mean?"

Aaron, no longer finding it necessary to whisper, said in a voice first hoarse, then closer to his normal pitch but with tenorial overtone, "Oh, no. We couldn't do that."

"Especially since you're here to dump it."

"Take it," Lolly pleaded. "Save it from a fate worse—"

"For a pig, there's only one fate." Kitty drew her index finger across her throat.

"Oh, don't say that." Aaron was horrified.

"And don't do that." Lolly shuddered.

Kitty, to make manifest the radical changes marriage had wrought in her life, called over to her husband, who had just shoveled the inconvenient flop off the bed of the truck onto the pebbled ground. "Kieran, do we want a pig? It's a lesbian."

"Which pig? That pig?"

"Yes. That pig."

"How can it be a lesbian?"

"Don't ask me. Ask God. She's the one should take full credit."

Lolly exchanged pleading for a lesson in etiquette. "It's a wedding present. You can't return it."

Kieran jumped down and scooped the manure back onto the shovel. "Then we should have had it for the wedding feast. But you'd taken it home with you." He paused. "Of course we could always use a bit of bacon."

"You wouldn't!" cried Lolly.

"If he wouldn't," said Kitty, "I would."

Lolly turned her pitiful gaze toward her husband. "Maybe we could build a separate pen. And maybe put a sow or two in with it from time to time."

"Well." Aaron breathed in and breathed out. "If that's what you prefer."

"It's not what I prefer. It's what I'm being forced to do," Lolly said, as Aaron reached over and put his hand on her shoulder. "Look at it," she added. "Look at how it wants to be here."

Kitty looked in the direction Lolly's out-thrust hand demanded. There was the pig, standing transfixed near the castle terrace, its gaze focused on the second-floor gallery that ran above the great hall. It didn't move, a rare moment for this particular animal.

"See?" said Aaron. "It likes the castle."

Kieran yelled back from the pasture where the flop was being recycled to improve—if such were possible—the planet's greenest grass. "Sure. And I like Dockery's pub, but that doesn't mean they're going to let me live there."

Kitty raised her hand, demanding silence. Aaron was relieved, since he had no answer to what Kieran had said and didn't want to say something stupid in front of his wife. Lolly moved closer to him, a show of solidarity for the verdict about to be handed down. They both looked at Kitty, who was now staring at the castle.

"Who's that in the window the pig's so interested in?" Kitty asked.

"What window?" Aaron squinted to hide his lack of interest.

"I think you mean *which* window," said Kitty.

Aaron didn't flinch. "Which window?"

"There above the great hall, the gallery, the second window from the left. The man standing there."

"What man?"

"The second window. The young man watching us. Brown jacket."

Lolly shook her head. "I don't see any brown jacket."

"Then get the hair out of your eyes. He's there; he's wearing a brown jacket and looking at us, and the pig's looking at him."

"Kitty," Aaron said, "I'm confused. I don't see a man with or without a brown jacket. In the second, third, or fourth window."

"Are the pig and I the only ones not blind, then?"

Lolly stretched her neck outward, Aaron crinkled his nose, each straining for a closer look. Kieran ignored the entire exchange and with noisy emphasis shoved the ramp back onto the bed of the truck.

"There," Kitty said. "Now he's gone, so don't even bother."

The pig clattered onto the terrace and began snuffling among the uneven stones.

Kitty gave a short laugh. "He must be one of the squatters come back for something left behind. We threw out all the bottles and filthy mattresses littered all over the place. They're in a heap in the far shed. But still inside is a loom. Up in the turret. And a harp with no strings. Would you believe the like? And a Ping-Pong table with paddles and Ping-Pong balls." She raised her head and yelled, "Don't take the Ping-Pong table. Or the loom or the harp. We'll buy them from you." She stopped. "There he is again, at the other window, at the end. Now can you see him?"

Again Lolly and Aaron looked.

"I still can't see him," said Lolly.

"Kitty," said Aaron, "there's no one there. You're seeing shadows, or maybe a mist is coming up."

"I'm seeing one of the squatters. And I'm going to go bargain with him."

Kieran busied himself with securing the back of the truck. "Do you want me to go with?"

"No need. If he's not as skinny as he looked, maybe he'd like a job. Help with the repairs they never finished. Like thatching the sheds."

Kieran gave the tailgate a good rattle. "I don't need any help. If I can't take care of a castle and a few cows and do a bit of roofing—with slate—"

"With thatch!" Kitty inserted, reviving a previously stated preference.

"To be discussed another time," Kieran concluded. "For now, don't expect me to train an apprentice in work you have to learn from the day you were born."

How fine he is, thought Kitty. Just like me: stubborn. Her impulse was simply to stand and admire her husband, but she knew that would unnerve him. "He's as good as hired," said Kitty. Then, to goad her husband into another point of contention, she added, "And we'll keep the pig. It is, after all, the one being besides myself has eyesight enough to see what's there for anyone to see." She swept past them all, moving with elegant determination toward the castle. Raising her right arm, she waved at the young man in the window. That he failed to wave back distressed her not at all. That he simply vanished gave her only the slightest pause.

She stepped onto the terrace. As she passed through the

heavy doors into the great hall, the pig followed, but stopped in the middle of the vast room and stared into a corner at the far end. There in the shadows was the young man, cap in hand. He wore a brown, crude-weave jacket over a tunic cinched with a cord that looked like rope. His pants legs went just below the knee. His feet were bare. He was looking at the pig, his brown eyes mournful yet expectant, his mouth and his entire face taut as if preparing themselves for whatever might happen.

"There you are." Kitty took a step forward. "I'm Kitty McCloud. I've taken the place, as you probably know. You're one of the squatters. I'm offering you a job, if you'd like."

She spoke to him in Irish, the language the squatters had come from Cork to learn. But he made no response; then ceased to be where he had been. He had simply disappeared. Kitty herself, unmoving, did not take her eyes off the spot where the youth had stood. She blinked twice, then said in a whisper, "Well, then; I guess he doesn't want the job." The pig sent out from behind a parabola of urine to water the flag-stone floor. It was then that Kitty remembered where she'd seen the young man before. At her wedding feast.

Afterword
by Carl Lennertz

Joe Caldwell's *The Pig Did It* is proof positive that word-of-mouth is alive and well, and thank goodness that still matters in this Twitter world—and by an author who doesn't own a computer and who doesn't drive.

Which is where and why I come in: my role as driver for a road trip with Joe, so he could do a string of bookstore readings, superseding my part in helping to market his book, a marvelous Irish comedy mystery/mystery comedy.

Joe Caldwell wrote several novels and plays after his arrival in New York City from Milwaukee in the Fifties. He endured that Manhattan christening known as the tiny walk-up apartment; he told me he could touch the Brooklyn Bridge foundation from the roof of his building. He also paid the bills as a writing teacher and by serving as a writer for that cultural TV phenomenon known as *Dark Shadows*. One of many anecdotes that Joe shared during our drive was that he and a co-writer wrote the character, Barnabus, on deadline one summer day. Barnabus. The reluctant vampire.

"Joe, now you tell me you wrote a vampire character a decade before Anne Rice and decades before Stephanie Meyers?!" I almost drove off the highway. We were en route to his last reading on the road trip.

"Well, I guess I did," Joe trilled in that delightful rasp of his. He sat perched in the passenger seat of my mini-van as we talked poetry and theater, politics and the state of the world. He was enjoying this "overnight" success at the age of eighty, and he was so grateful for the people who turned out for his readings, and for the booksellers who hosted him in their beautiful stores.

Ah, bookstores. Therein lies the secret of *The Pig Did It.* First, Barnes & Noble tapped it as a Discover Pick, and then independent bookstore owners in disparate parts of the country embraced it. They would email me excitedly, reporting that they had personally handsold twenty, thirty, eighty copies!

While never a bestseller in the strict sense of the word, the book just kept finding new fans—in the form of a full-page *Washington Post Book World* rave to bulk purchases by literary mail-order catalogs. But mostly, the word-of-mouth engine in book groups and bookstores just kept chugging along, and now five years since the book's hardcover publication, we need to print more copies of the paperback yet again. The 11th printing, which is wonderful. And we're dubbing this the 5th Anniversary edition.

And all for a book that Joe wrote as a break from his self-described dark novels about sex and death. As he told an audience at New York's Three Lives Bookstore during his inaugural reading: "I wanted to write something fun, to write more about family and romance. And now, looking back at the final book, I see that it, too, is about sex and death!"

So there we have it. Sex. Death. A comedy? A mystery? Did the pig do it? Even as you read this after finishing the book, you may still be wondering about the role of the pig in the lives of Aaron, Kitty, Declan, and the others. And Joe's Irish journey continues in two sequels.

And I find I want to fire up the van and take Joe around to visit more bookstores again on a 5th anniversary tour. Joe would absolutely love the silliness of the silk tour jacket that I plan to obtain for him. Size small, heart big.

People love Joe, the book, the pig, his marvelous tale.